DJUSD
Public Schools
Library Protection Act 1998

Raven of the Waves

Also by Michael Cadnum

IN A DARK WOOD

Raven of the Waves

by Michael Cadnum

Orchard Books / New York
An Imprint of Scholastic Inc.

Orchard Books, an imprint of Scholastic Inc.
95 Madison Avenue, New York, NY 10016

Manufactured in the United States of America
Book design by Vicki Fischman
The text of this book is set in 11 point Caslon.

10 9 8 7 6 5 4 3 2 1

Library of Congress Cataloging-in-Publication Data
Cadnum, Michael.
Raven of the waves / by Michael Cadnum.
    p.   cm.
Summary: On his first Viking raid, seventeen-year-old Lidsmod sails
on the ship Raven, joining his comrades as they destroy and plunder
villages in medieval England and take an Anglo-Saxon boy as captive.
ISBN 0-531-30334-9
1.Vikings—Juvenile fiction. [1. Vikings—Fiction. 2. Anglo-Saxons—
Fiction. 3. Great Britain—History—Anglo-Saxon period, 449–1066—
Fiction.] I. Title.
PZ7.C11724 Rav 2001 [Fic]—dc21 00-64986

FOR SHERINA

Faith shall wing farther, heart higher
Hope nearer Heaven as night falls.

—from *Aethelwulf's Hymn*

794 A.D.

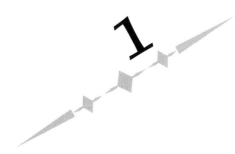

THE FJORD WAS CALM, the high cliffs and the ships' prows mirrored in the blue.

Lidsmod turned back to Gunnar, trying to hide his disappointment.

Gunnar smiled sympathetically and put a hand on the young man's shoulder. "You know how much we would like you to sail with us," he said.

At seventeen Lidsmod was old enough to take an oar in a warship. But the voyage was fully manned, and Gunnar had refused permission to older and more experienced shipmates than Lidsmod.

"Come on, you two," Opir cried from the distance. "You'll be late!"

Gunnar waved but stayed where he was.

Lidsmod straightened his back and looked the tall, tanned Gunnar in the eye. "I understand, Gunnar," he managed to say. He added the old blessing, "May the gods blind every foe."

Gunnar smiled. "I would be grateful to have the son of Fastivi in my ship, especially on a fighting voyage like this."

"We'll be late for the horse fight," said Lidsmod.

"It was a bad idea to have a horse fight the day before our three ships sail," sighed Gunnar. "But no one can tell these men what to do."

Like all the other villagers of Spjothof, Lidsmod was very curious whether Gorm's stallion would be able to finish this fight as quickly as he had the other two that spring. Gorm's horse was right out of Odin's heart if there ever were such a beast. The other men had been gleeful with excitement. There had not been such a day in years—three ships taking to sea to find gold, and a horse fight and an ale feast to wish them well.

But Lidsmod stayed a few moments longer beside the new ship *Raven,* her keel scar on sand down to where she rode the still water, the chests packed, the mast seated on its supports. The pine oars gave off a subtle perfume so fine that Lidsmod wanted to lie down in the ship and stare up at the sky.

He loved this ship, as the other men loved theirs, bold *Crane*—its handsome bird's head just repainted, and the famous sea-blackened *Landwaster* farther along—the ship that once had taken the heads of five hundred Danes. To have such a famous ship on a journey was enough to make the sword bright, but Lidsmod admired *Raven,* this newest, keenest ship he had watched Njord hew from tall, white-fleshed trees.

Njord the shipwright strode across the beach, years of wood tar on his stiff leather apron. "You two don't want to see the fight?"

"I wouldn't miss it," said Gunnar sardonically.

"I prefer ships to horses too," said Njord, and the two men laughed.

Njord nodded at Lidsmod, offering a sympathetic smile.

4

I must learn to hide my thoughts, thought Lidsmod. Fighting men show no feelings.

"I know you don't want trouble," Njord said. His hair was white, like the wing of a tern, his face wrinkled. "Men bet silver, lose, and carry the hard feelings for a long time, even on a voyage to great fortune."

From far off came the excited, lustful whistle of the mare, and the answering nicker of one of the stallions.

The entire village of Spjothof was gathered. The little farming village at the end of the fjord had stopped everything to celebrate the most exciting day since *Landwaster* had returned with Danish gold five summers before.

Lidsmod took his place among the crowd, and he was not sorry he was here. These were his friends, men and women he had known all his life. Lidsmod's mother, Fastivi, had a place of honor at the front of the crowd, her golden hair touched with gray. Lidsmod joined her, the crowd settling around them, clapping and calling excitedly.

Everyone in the village knew how Fastivi had discovered a bear over the torn body of her husband, when Lidsmod was a few months old. Wearing her infant son lashed to her back, safely swaddled, she had seized her husband's spear and killed the beast with one thrust, through hide and heart. Some villagers believed that it had not been a bear at all, but an apparition—Odin in disguise to test the courage of this beautiful woman.

The mare was tethered, jerking the walrus-hide rope. Her eyes were wild, and she danced, fighting to break what held her because she could smell the stallions.

The villagers' cheeks were berry bright and the sunlight was warm for the first time in many months. Everyone stood next to a friend or behind a companion he could clap on a shoulder. Opir hooted and laughed, the sound enough to make any man or woman laugh in turn.

Only Torsten stood alone, arms folded. He watched the fighting pit with hard gray eyes. He watched the crowd. He eyed the women. There was always a space around Torsten—he wore a sword even now. No man spoke to Torsten, and Torsten rarely spoke.

Gorm pulled Ice Lightning into the fighting pit and loosed both the hood and the rope. The horse ran as if in the far pasture, and then it scented the mare, safe behind the fence of pine spears. Gorm lifted his staff, his neighbors cheering. Ice Lightning tossed, fought the air, kicked at the sun. The frisky stallion was still shaggy with winter, and when he kicked, drifts of gray hair came free and glittered in the sunlight. He was all one color, like dirty snow.

And then came the challenger, Floki's horse, Biter, brown as seasoned oak and strong. Biter had gained the villagers' admiration but no bettors. Both horses were compact, stout, hairy, and quick. They did not stand on earth but on air, dancing.

Both stallions saw each other now and scented the mare. She thundered her hind hooves against the pine fence.

"She wants both of them at once," called Opir, and people laughed.

Then the crowd was silent. Lidsmod wondered if human battle was like this, the air before the fight so still, the sun so bright.

Biter charged the ice gray stallion, and the horse sprawled.

Gorm stabbed at his horse with his staff, but missed because Ice Lightning was up so quickly. Floki cheered his horse, but the crowd roared with him so loudly, no one could hear the voice of one man. A bright red crescent appeared in Biter's neck, and just as suddenly Ice Lightning's coat was pink on his forelegs, and blood and spit flew into the air. The two stallions shrieked—a furious, terrible sound—and then, at once, they were both down.

Mud flew, and hooves thudded turf, slashed it, ripped dirt, and the horses rose again, two necks knotted together, strips of hide dangling. The two horse handlers stood poised, spectators now, their staves unneeded.

Then the middle period of the fight began, as it will when men are wrestling, bets placed on market day. The first excitement gone, the long, grinding work was under way. Horse hair was spiky with sweat. The two horses grunted.

Opir shook his fist and jumped up and down so the men around him laughed, and even tall, long-haired Gunnar folded his arms and called out. This was a fight indeed. No one had guessed that Gorm's pale, powerful horse would have so much trouble. Njord shook both fists in the air. Some men began to bet on the brown stallion, the stocky, hard-fighting Biter. Men began to call Biter's name. Even if Biter lost, he would die with his name in song, truly nameworthy. Biter, ale drinkers would sing, the brave horse who flew at Ice Lightning.

Men put their heads together. Women cheered and talked among themselves and to the men near them.

Biter was the younger horse, some said. Ice Lightning had been in too many fights. He had not rested enough. He had not trained.

Lidsmod cheered too, proud to see such fighting courage.

Gorm's hands found new places on his staff, and his jaw muscles bunched. He whacked Ice Lightning three times, but the horse could not fight harder. The cords in the horse's neck stood out, and the veins too, his eyes wide, his teeth buried in Biter's mane.

Biter wheeled, struggling to shake loose the snow gray horse and reach him with his hind hooves. He escaped at last, at the cost of leaving a half-moon chunk of his flesh in Ice Lightning's teeth.

Perhaps Ice Lightning believed all along he would defeat this new horse, this tough young stallion. Or perhaps the taste of Biter's blood in his mouth gave him confidence, bad confidence, the kind that leads to error.

People would murmur about it afterward. What happened to Gorm's horse? Why did it make its mistake? But no one would be able to say for certain because, after all, probably even horses were subject to the powers of the Norns, the weavers of destiny.

The stallions grappled. Biter spun, free of Ice Lightning. Ice Lightning did not press and find a new tooth hold, nor did he rear and prance away. He did nothing for the space of a long breath. Then Biter turned and shot a rear hoof to Ice Lightning's head.

There was a crack, a sickening snap.

Ice Lightning was down.

He was lying on the scarred grass, eyes open, ribs bellowing in and out, his hooves still.

The villagers cheered. Opir leaped up and down, his voice louder than any other. Lidsmod cheered too, but he was sorry to see the veteran stallion so badly hurt.

Gorm threw down his staff. His eyes had no expression, and his hands were at his belt.

Lidsmod saw it clearly, because even when he was feasting or drunk on the deepest ale, it seemed to Lidsmod that some part of him was wide awake. He saw Gorm with the knife in his hand. Gorm stepped to the side of Biter, and Lidsmod understood at once what Gorm was about to do.

Lidsmod lunged through the crowd and reached for Gorm's knife.

2

TOO LATE.

Gorm's herring-quick blade slipped into the brown horse and opened a long, red gash.

A groan rose from every mouth, then there was silence. Lidsmod did not dare strike Gorm, a sun-bronzed fighting man with long, tallow yellow hair. Gorm held the bloody blade before Lidsmod's eyes, and Lidsmod was certain its point would prick out his sight. And yet Lidsmod stayed where he was, shielding the struggling horse as the animal sagged, slumped, and fell into its own widening sea of blood.

Gunnar gripped Gorm by the hair of his head. "Help me," the sea chief said to Lidsmod, and the young man helped heave the struggling Gorm through the parting crowd of villagers. Behind them men struggled to keep the anguished Floki from reaching Gorm.

Biter panted and shivered, struggling to his feet; his intestines slipped from the cut. Njord lifted his peg mallet, the one he had used for the godpins in *Raven*'s prow, and brought it down on the horse's skull. Then he patted the neck of the fallen victor.

Eirik began to sing a poem. It was an old verse, about a horse that belonged to Odin—beyond even the last battle, running forever under the blue sky. Eirik was a mighty skald, a poet. He began to chant a new song, one that celebrated a familiar truth: men and beasts both fall. The triumph is in the battle, not the victory.

The feast began very quietly. The villagers filed into the long hall without joy. Wooden plates clattered. Women whispered, men looked straight ahead and did not speak.

Lidsmod could not eat, but not only because of the blood he had seen. Blood was salt water, Lidsmod tried to tell himself, nothing more. It was the injustice of it that gnawed at him. Lidsmod stared at his mutton. Gorm owed a great price for the loss of such a horse, Lidsmod knew. This was how things were for men and horses. The loom squeaked, and the Dark Weavers tricked a man into a new pattern, and he was helpless.

"Not hungry, Lidsmod?" said Opir. "I can always eat. I eat. I laugh. Floki will have Gorm's skin," said Opir, sucking fat off his fingers. "Or every ewe he owns. Don't worry."

"Gorm shouldn't come with us," said Ulf, a massive, bald warrior staring at the wooden table before him.

"He's a good fighter," said Opir. "There is no one quite like him. Except for me, of course." Opir's name meant "Boaster." He made high claims for himself, but it was hard to tell how seriously.

"Gorm will have to pay a great price," said Ulf. That was the only way men could begin to balance the great unfairness of the world. By giving a price to things, man or beast, misfortune could be offset.

Word began to escape the jarl's hall. Negotiations were well begun. Floki had agreed that twenty of Gorm's finest ewes would be a good payment for the horse. It was a formal situation, and despite the emotion between the two men, if it were resolved now and payment established, the matter would be finished and all could go on with their lives.

"The heart loss cannot be paid for," said the broad-shouldered Ulf sadly, drinking hard at his ale.

Then word stirred the hall that Gorm would have to pay ten rams and more for the sorrow he had caused.

"Agree," said the jarl. "Or stay here all summer, tending pigs. Many good men will do the same."

In the jarl's hall, Gorm couldn't speak. He hated this village, this empty, hungry place. If it weren't so poor, so overcrowded, there would be no need for journeys. Gorm was the youngest son of four brothers. What did life hold for him? Life had cheated him from the start. The three ships would need Gorm's quick sword when they touched keel to sand. Then they would say, "Where's Gorm, to help us with his steady hand?"

But to be stalwart and trustworthy—that was more important to the men of Spjothof than skill with a sword. A man's temperament, what he was like during long, salt-gritty nights, that was what mattered.

So Gorm had to pretend. "It was wrong to cut the horse," he said to the jarl. "I should not have done it. Twenty ewes and ten rams. I agree."

Word spread into the feasting hall, and when Gorm

and the ranking men of the village entered there was a special kind of cheer, like a sigh.

It was a great feast, with much drinking. Fastivi sat beside Gunnar, her long gold and silver hair tied back. Gunnar had told Lidsmod that of all the men he had known, Leif, Lidsmod's father, had sung with the finest voice. It was a gift, such a voice, and even now the village remembered it with reverence.

Only Torsten was not drinking. Men and women recalled the old song sagas: the Theft of the Horses from the Danish Cave, or the Horses of Ragnarok, the Doom Battle of the gods. But Torsten sat alone, a stout, still figure with a long, uncombed beard.

The bench beside Lidsmod shook, and Opir belched as he settled himself. "My good Lidsmod, look happy. You'll stay here with all these beautiful women, and no one else as handsome as you to distract them. You'll be sore in all the right places, Lidsmod. Don't let them wear you out."

Lidsmod blushed. Talk of the trip made his heart sink, but at the same time he knew Hallgerd, the jarl's daughter, was watching. What if she could hear what Opir was saying!

"Who'll row with Torsten?" asked Lidsmod to change the subject.

Opir gazed into his ale cup. "Torsten has surprised everyone. He's decided to row in *Raven*. When I stride past Torsten, Torsten shivers! When I speak to Torsten, Torsten looks down like a maiden." All of this was said in a low voice, with Opir glancing up to make sure that Torsten could not hear.

Lidsmod asked, in a keen whisper, "Did you see Torsten against the Danes?"

Opir smiled and slapped the table. "Come along, Lidsmod, eat your supper." He used the word for a night meal, *nattverdr*, making his voice that of a mother coaxing a child.

Lidsmod persisted. "What is Torsten like—in battle?"

Opir did not answer at once. Soon Eirik would sing, and the jarl would offer words to Odin, and Opir would lead the merry ale faces in a cheerful song. Then they would all listen to a feasting saga from Eirik, perhaps of a bear the size of an iceberg, or of a fiery serpent from beneath the sea. Ale tales, nothing to turn a tear or remind a man scarred to the bone what the sea trail was really like.

"Torsten is a berserker," said Opir at last.

"I'll never be able to see Torsten fight, myself," Lidsmod said, trying to sound as though this did not matter to him.

"And you think that a great shame, don't you, Lidsmod! Better you should see the world as it is—fjord and sky. And men as they are—some good, some not so good. If you have any luck, you will never see what a berserker can do."

Just then Hego ran into the feasting hall to say the sky was showering like burning straw, and the crowd streamed forth into the cold night to see. In the rush, Hego—a slow-witted man, who loved mead as he loved life—tripped over the threshold and fell hard on his face.

3

THE NEXT MORNING the village was very quiet except for Njord's men, boatbuilders who could wield mallets and tighten ropes even with the worst mead headaches.

The night before Lidsmod had gaped at the great rain of fire from the heavens, a wonderful omen, the spectacle over all too quickly. Now he was up early to see the ships go off on their voyage, his head thick with last night's drinking, the sunlight serene and bright off the fjord. Sheep stirred in their pens. The echoes of hammering resounded off the high cliffs, and morning smoke drifted over the water from cooking fires.

Hego stood by the fjord, hiding his face, gazing off at the perfect, still water. The stones beside the path were splashed with lichen and bright green moss. Gunnar put his arm around Lidsmod and said, "I have some news for you."

Lidsmod was filled with the farewells he was about to offer to the departing fighting men. He did not speak.

"The village loves Hego," Gunnar said.

Lidsmod knew this was true enough but did not understand why this was news. A person like Hego was close to some truth about the weft of things. Odin himself

15

had given one of his eyes so that he could drink from the Well of Wisdom. Hego's wits had been taken years ago in exchange for something, too—kindness, and a steady, childlike nature. And yet, Hego's strength was undoubted—he could flense a walrus all by himself.

"He'll make a good shipmate," Lidsmod said.

"Every sign has been good, for weeks," said Gunnar. "The fulmars were seen winging north, and last week Egil saw a whale, playing like a seal in the mouth of the fjord." Spring had come on hard, like a beast in rut, and the scum ice had aged and melted as men looked on from their *knorrs,* low in the water from their cargo. "Go speak to Hego."

Mystified, Lidsmod called to Hego, but the tall man turned his face resolutely away.

Lidsmod took Hego's arm. And saw what was wrong.

The fall outside the mead hall had been brutal. Hego's eyes were slits in a swollen, bruised face.

Gunnar joined them at the water's edge. "Can you see out of those eyes, good Hego?" said Gunnar gently.

"I can see the feathers on a fox," countered Hego lugubriously, an old phrase describing unnaturally acute eyesight.

"Do you see the piglet that's gotten loose, and runs along the shore?" asked Gunnar.

There was no escaped pig. Lidsmod caught Gunnar's eye and bit his lip.

"Of course I can," said Hego.

"You are the village's liveliest spirit," said Gunnar kindly. "The geese would be restless without you, and the milk would curdle."

16

Lidsmod tried to make himself just a little taller and lifted his chin so that he might resemble a strong, calm man of power.

Gunnar whispered in Hego's ear and patted the man's arm. Then Gunnar strode along the shore to the ships and called to Njord. Lidsmod followed, forbidding himself to feel hope. Gunnar said, "Hego will stay here."

"He'll be missed," said Njord. "His back is as strong as his head is empty."

Gunnar said, "Lidsmod goes in his place."

Njord's creased face folded into a smile. "Our young Lidsmod, taking a chance at seafaring. Are you ready to earn a sword and shield, lad?"

"With the help of Thor," began Lidsmod, not wanting to appear too eager, and not wanting to offend the gods with the pride and hope that made his voice a rasp.

Njord laughed. "With the help of your shipmates, you mean."

Eirik was singing as he packed his sea chest, the tune about the giants at the edges of the earth.

Gunnar gave Lidsmod a mock scowl. "Don't stand there gawking. Run and say good-bye to your mother."

"You'll bring back gold," Fastivi said to her son.

"The stories are that there are halls filled with gold and silver. Lying there, like elf treasure," Lidsmod said.

"What sort of men would leave gold lying around with no one to guard it?"

"Men it's lucky to discover."

Lidsmod's mother laughed, but then they both fell silent.

"They are not good fighting men?" she asked.

"Even worse than the Danes." But the Danes could be fierce. Many men from Spjothof had come back from Dane battles with their bodies red as runes with sword cuts. Spjothof was far north of the land of Danes, in a country everyone referred to simply as Northland, or Norge. "They don't know battle at all, these Westland men. They are like children."

Word had arrived on a *knorr,* a freight ship, in late summer the year before. A great raid, fifty ships or more, had fallen upon the Westland, and taken gold from men who would not fight. Much gold—goblets, shepherd's crooks, and jewels, too, like the emeralds and sapphires traders carried out of the Mediterranean, that sea of legend.

The men and boys of Spjothof had stirred. Spjothof meant "spear hall." At one time, in the days of the sagas, it had been a village of warriors who could farm and fight off Danes and prosper. Now there were too many sons without inheritance after the eldest was satisfied, and all the men were restless. Sometimes a raid on the Danes was organized, but the Danes were difficult prey. *Landwaster* had burned three villages years before, and Ulf had come back wolf coated, with a prized fur that had belonged to a Danish king. There were many songs about this ship and its summer of fire. But there was need for another such summer, and soon.

"You will come back with jarls in chains," Fastivi said. "We'll keep them as slaves. We will gather ransom for many years."

Lidsmod's mother was a brave woman, tall and handsome, but he could hear the anxiety she did so much to hide. "I'll come back with whole chains of silver," he said, trying his best to sound sure.

His mother turned away. She opened a shutter to let in the bright sunlight. "Tell these men-like-children that we value their gold more than they do. If they won't look after it, they deserve to lose it to better men."

"I'll tell them that. I'm sure it will cheer them."

Fastivi gave her son a smile that, she believed, hid her feelings entirely. Many summers ago her husband, Leif, had been killed by a yearling bear, and killing the beast had been a simple matter, as filled with fury and grief as she had been. She had killed the young bear and let the stream of ice melt carry the carcass away. The legends of her courage were merely fireside songs. Gunnar had been kind, and he was a good man, but she still mourned her husband.

"Go down to the ship," she said. "I'll stand where you can see me as you sail."

Lidsmod hugged her and then left, hurrying into the daylight.

It was cruel that a son should go down to sea. But she wanted him to be a man of *virding,* of worth. She was proud of Gunnar's request. Every woman would watch her as she passed by, and know her pride.

So soon a man, Fastivi thought. She trembled, and closed her eyes. But there were only three tears. Only three. Odin would remember. Sorrow would be repaid with joy.

For a long time she stood still, the song in her heart the song of Odin's ravens—his scouts—as they searched the world on behalf of the one-eyed god. The song was a prayer that no steel would touch her son, and that the mountains of the sea would fall away before him.

The three ships made dark cuts in the fjord. The water was perfect blue, unstained by a ripple. The fjord looked like a long, crooked sword. Lidsmod saw how perfect everything was, and how quiet. Men worked, taking their places. Nearly all the men of Spjothof were there, and their work took little speech.

"I feel as fit as a hundred men," said Opir, standing by the shore. "My head does not hurt. I have held every sip of ale in my belly, and never vomited in my life."

Men fastened, tied, tucked.

"I can drink a river of ale to the bottom, and then eat the fish," said Opir.

Men ignored him, not unkindly.

"I'm ready to row with the stoutest," Opir continued. "Thor could not outrow me this morning." He stepped to the water and vomited. "My gift to the children of Loki," said Opir.

Gunnar caught Opir's eye. He did not have to speak. Opir silenced himself and scrambled into *Raven*.

Lidsmod's friends gathered him into *Raven* with their strong arms. Ulf patted the chest top beside him, the storage place for food and weapons. Lidsmod took the pine oar in his grip, beside the hairy hands of Ulf.

Lidsmod glanced up to wave to his mother. Fastivi was standing far up the beach, a dark-cloaked figure with bright hair. Then Lidsmod's eyes were wet with a new cause, one he did not want to share with his shipmates. Hallgerd was waving too, and there could be no question.

The beautiful daughter of the jarl was calling Lidsmod's name, and waving. Could there be tears in her eyes?

In a rush, the oars were in the water, and *Raven* lifted her head, alive.

Their way was quick. The other two ships lingered behind, *Crane* and the black *Landwaster. Raven* was the fastest. The water rushed beneath the planks at Lidsmod's feet. He could feel it rushing, like the rapids of a mountain stream.

As they rowed, Ulf glanced over at Lidsmod and smiled with his white teeth in his golden beard. Lidsmod could not believe his good fortune.

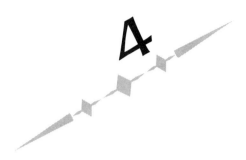

WIGLAF HURRIED, leaving the shadows of the monastery.

He scurried past the stonemasons, gray rocks piled around, surrounded by bright yellow straw to soak up the spring damp. Saint John's Church was going to be dwarfed by its own tower someday, when the effort was complete.

Stag the hound trailed Wiglaf into the village, along the north-south street, but he followed the straight route only briefly. The dog had flushed out a mouse, and he scampered, zigzagging, tearing at the ground when he scented the mouse's hiding place.

Wiglaf had been told this road led all the way to the city if a traveler walked straight on and did not fall to mischief on the way. The road was rutted from oxcart wheels, a family of ducks swimming one of the long, deep puddles. Far at the end of town was Beornbold, the shield hall, where Lord Redwald stayed when he was in his home. The hall was full of armed men whose ale rations arrived from upriver on barges, great barrels of it; sword bearers were rarely sober, according to Aethelwulf.

Stag looked up at Wiglaf at the sound of his name and left the torn-up earth where a mouse now had a story to tell to his rodent kin. Wiglaf ran through the village, toward the river and the homestead where he had learned to walk and say his prayers.

Aethelwulf, probably the kindest and wisest man in the land where the English tongue was spoken, had sent Wiglaf on an errand to seek a cockerel, a fine young rooster, for the evening meal this night. Wiglaf was excited about seeing his father and his brothers; it had been weeks since he had visited the cottage where he had been born, even though it was a short distance away, little more than two long bow shots.

But when Wiglaf saw his brothers at last, he did not want to make a sound—there was serious trouble.

Their bull was trapped in the river, an ancient, horrible, spotted bull that always rolled its eye at Wiglaf. The twins pulled at the rope, calling to the brute. They were strong young men, stocky, and slimed with mud. The bull lifted his muzzle, dripping with water, and gave a long, angry bellow, pulling against the two. The bull had sired every calf between here and Hunlaf's village, and showed no wear from long seasons of servicing breed cows. The twins strained, but Wiglaf sensed they both had the same thought: if and when they dragged this beast from the water, what would this wet, furious monster do?

They dug their heels into the mud, slipped, and each found new places in the grass that had not yet been trodden to dirt soup. And at that point, as the warm spring rain was beginning again, their father arrived.

Sigemund had brought his mattock with him. He was always carrying this tool, half shovel, half peat chopper, when he was not carrying his wood ax. When he saw his two grown sons straining like men trying to unearth a stump, he shook his head.

The square-headed farmer caught sight of Wiglaf and gave a wry grin. "Look how they both stare back at me, Wiglaf," he said, giving his frail youngest son a rough pat. "Why has Jesus blessed me with such fools for sons? Twins, as though you needed two noses where one would do, or two rump holes instead of one."

Wiglaf's father flung aside the mattock, sending it deliberately into a hummock of grass and not into the mud, and strode toward the twins, giving them dramatic but not terribly accurate punches to the head. "Grab it, you two piss holes. No, leave it," he commanded. "I'll do it myself."

Wiglaf knew this was a test. His father had to prove that he was wise and strong-armed, but the bull was too willful. All the powers of the day and all the powers of the night could not help Sigemund drag this bull. The animal rolled its eyes. It fought the mud and it fought the rope and bellowed.

But Sigemund was stubborn. The dark-haired man pulled slowly, hand over hand. The bull threw up its hooves on all sides and floated, like a horse killed with bloat and only not dead yet, still looking around to say good-bye to the grass and the trees.

"We've got him," called Sigemund. "Come on, help me drag him. No don't, you two old women; I change my mind—get out of the way." Sigemund reasoned that a man of strength could drag a floating bull through the spring river or he might as well die. He fought the rope to an alder and took a turn around the trunk, tied a quick oxen knot, and then there was only the prayer that the tree—a good tree but little older than Wiglaf's thirteen years—would hold.

Sigemund spat. So with bulls, so with sons. He spat again and grinned at the bull, who rolled its eyes, afraid and angry. Sigemund laughed. "He's going to gut you for shoe straps," he hooted at his sons. He kicked one of the twins. "And right too."

The mattock was not muddy. Sigemund knew how to cast down a tool. Never in mud, never before God into water, and never so that someone in haste or as stupid as one of his sons might step on it and hurt themselves.

He turned back, and the twins were working at the rope, retying the knot. The hair along the bull's spine was tufted in fury. Sigemund leaned on the mattock and sighed, shaking his head at Wiglaf. "Forni and Edwin are much more stupid than I ever was. Strong, but what's strength compared to a bull?"

Wiglaf started to ask how the bull had escaped, and why it had tried to cross the river, but was sorry as soon as he opened his mouth because his father was examining him, eyeing his crippled arm, walking around behind him, as though appraising a piece of livestock.

"They feed you well enough, those churchmen?"

"Quite well enough, Father," said Wiglaf.

The bull started after the twins as they greeted Wiglaf, the two seventeen-year-olds scampering. The beast snorted, the two brothers dodging the great hooked horns. Stag, who had no reason to love horned creatures, shrank behind a dock bush with its large, lush leaves.

The bull reached the end of the rope. The alder tossed and straightened itself up again, and the bull, pulled sideways, collapsed. And was on his feet at once, strong and stupid, clawing mud with one hoof, and furious.

"Hush!" said Wiglaf's father. He leaned on the mattock and squinted, cupping a dirty hand behind one ear.

The twins quieted too at the approach of hoofbeats. Riders were rare here beside the river. Wiglaf recognized the horseman just as his father did.

"It can't be!" said Sigemund. "Lord Redwald is off as usual to Eoforwic, that city at the end of the world."

Wiglaf thought that the rider carried himself exactly like Lord Redwald, and wore Redwald's blue cloak, but did not say so.

"What if he's seen the foolishness with the bull?" said Wiglaf's father. The beast had nearly drowned through its own mischance, but what lord understood the ways of *wyrd*—fate? "Lord Redwald's always smiling," said Sigemund, "and a good giver of the ale at feasting tide, but you know how these *ealdormen* are, all song and ring gifts and no more sense than a cock sparrow."

Lord Redwald rode around a huge puddle, his horse picking its way through the sloppy mud.

"Besides, Redwald took away my youngest, Wiglaf. This was an unjust thing to do," said Sigemund, not unkindly, "when every lord should know that a strong fist to the head and a stout foot in the backside would pound a boy into manhood. Even a boy with a withered arm. Look at you, smarter than the twins put together."

Redwald approached, beaming, only a few flecks of mud on his deep blue cloak. Some men were wise and gentle, thought Wiglaf, like Father Aethelwulf. But some men had happy faces that cheered the heart, and Redwald was one.

"It's a good warm rain," said Redwald brightly.

"A good warm rain, my lord," said Sigemund.

"We are lucky to be here, Sigemund. The city is not a place for honest men."

Sigemund blinked. Not with the rain. The rain had just now stopped. Wiglaf sensed his father's attempt to match noble Angle speech with proper words of his own.

"It's true, my lord," said Wiglaf's father, "that Dunwic is a fine place with a good name."

Lord Redwald laughed. "I like talking to you, Sigemund. You have a wise tongue. But if you wanted to name things all over again, what would *you* call them?"

"Perhaps the animals would have new names, although there is no better word for dog than *hund*."

Dunwic was a small hamlet of hardworking peasants, with a smell of livestock in the cool air. And, of course, the abbey, with scaffolding rising like a tower's skeleton where, someday, there would be a stone edifice, the pride of God and man.

Sometimes Wiglaf was as happy as Lord Redwald seemed to be. Wiglaf loved this countryside. There was, he was certain, no better place under Heaven.

"The river isn't so high this year," said Redwald.

"No, not so high, my lord," Sigemund agreed.

"And it'll go down soon," said Redwald. His voice was a little less merry as he said this.

"Lord Redwald, pray, what does the river have to do with me?"

Redwald knew that Sigemund was a good farmer, and he knew the spark in his eye was a look of intelligence, but there was something untrustworthy about the man. He was a peasant, and entirely belonged with mud and hens and ox droppings. His wife—who looked like Sige-mund, as Sigemund looked like his sons, who in turn looked like each other—was missing all the teeth on her left side, the side where Sigemund's fist struck her jaw. It was common enough. Men struck their women. It was hardly a surprise.

But here was the bright youth Wiglaf, a lad for whom Redwald had paid good silver. It had to be done. An *ealdorman* had to take care of what belonged to him. His beasts, his men. An intelligent peasant boy could not be wasted.

So Lord Redwald had bought the boy three winters past, and now the boy studied at the abbey, enduring the abbot's scholarly habits, and learning also the holy man's gift with medicine. It was not merely kindness on Redwald's part. The abbot was old. The winters were harder every year. Another man in Dunwic with a touch for healing would be a blessing.

"The bull looks tired," said Redwald. "And ill-tempered. He's rolling his eyes and digging a trough with his hoof. I saw several dead sheep floating by me in the river today. Tumbling over and over. It's surprising how animals end up in the river and drown."

"They have no more sense than some people, Lord Redwald." The peasant's eyes looked aside for an instant, and then looked back at Redwald with new intensity. "But even at flood time it takes a very unlucky beast to end up in the river."

Like most of the folk of Dunwic, Sigemund loved to talk. Redwald leaned down. "Has the bull been in the water?"

"No, my lord."

"Not at all?"

"Not far in," said Sigemund. "Only a short way in," he added. "Only for a swim and then out again on his own with no trouble to any of us."

"None of us seek trouble," said Lord Redwald.

Wiglaf caught something in the nobleman's tone.

"Whatever God wills, my lord," said Wiglaf's father.

"You and your twin sons always have an ax close by?" said Lord Redwald. It was less question than statement.

"Or mattock, or hammer," said Wiglaf's father. "We have a weapon against beast or devil all day long, my lord."

"And you keep an eye on the river, like good men," said Lord Redwald.

Wiglaf knew that his father never so much as skipped a stone on the river. Farmers took little notice of mud hens or river barges. The river that flowed past Dunwic was called affectionately the Ooze, if village folk referred to it at all.

"Why, my lord," said Sigemund, "if I may ask?"

For a peasant to ask a direct question of a lord was close to insubordination, and Wiglaf could not look at the alert, insolent expression on his father's face.

The lord gave Wiglaf a thoughtful smile and gazed at the gray-green horizon to the south.

He rode off without answering.

5

WIGLAF WAS LATE, and Aethelwulf was worried.

When the abbot had stepped out earlier that afternoon to observe the stonemasons' progress, he had seen a fox at the edge of the woods. The vixen, with hair as bright as Lord Redwald's, was brazen, cutting a way through the tall grass the sheep had not yet been allowed to touch.

In his younger years Aethelwulf had been the most foul-tempered of Christian men. He had chosen a life as a man of faith because he was too surly to deal with bread eaters, as servants were called. He wanted books and quiet. And now in this tiny monastery, with a scant seven brothers and the boy to help with the sheep and to listen to him prattle his medical lore, which leaves could kill and which could cure, he was growing timid as well.

Every peasant knew that a fox was a potent omen, but as a man of learning he should have been more skeptical. The abbot made the sign of the holy cross and clapped his hands three times. The vixen froze and looked at Aethelwulf.

It was like the glance of the very Devil.

Aethelwulf stooped to pick up a stone, sharp and heavy. The beast vanished.

The masons were slow-working fellows, city men accustomed to cow's cheese at every meal. They liked to stand, arms folded, admiring their progress. Aethelwulf found himself more patient than he would have been in earlier years, understanding that skilled laboring men must proceed with care. They had constructed a circular trough for the mixing of mortar, the mortar mill worked by two men walking a slow circle. Some stones were already in place, to show how grand the tower would be when the masons decided to labor as well as they planned.

But not even the deliberate speech of the masons could irritate him, the foreman indicating, in his methodical way, that there the scaffolding would rise further, and here the stone chips would gather—things the abbot could clearly see for himself.

"All is as it should be," said the lead mason gently but emphatically, the way some men of town and village spoke to priests, as though church folk were saintly but slightly simple, ignorant of the real world.

Aethelwulf smiled, bland and understanding. "Good work, men," he heard himself say. He returned to his studies, marveling at himself. Since when was he so patient? It was all the influence of Wiglaf—there could be no question.

And Wiglaf was late.

When a hound had been found near the henhouse a few months past, so badly slashed by a stag's antlers that its jaw hung like bloody flap, none of the brothers would touch it. But Wiglaf had marched up to the strange hound, put a hand on it, and told it that all would be well.

Father Aethelwulf had never cured a dog, but the boy's faith in him gave the abbot a taste of God's faith in man, and so Aethelwulf bound the jaw with linen and devised a funnel so that the boy could feed the hound raw eggs. The jaw had healed crooked, and the dog had a lopsided sneer no matter what it was feeling, boredom or happiness. The boy called it Stag, with a sort of logic the great learned man Bede no doubt would have found hard to follow, but which Aethelwulf, with his ever weaker mind, quite understood.

Now Aethelwulf sat reading the treatise on the Sphere of Apuleius, a formula used to foretell the outcome of an illness. At least, he was trying to read. It was an easy concept to understand. The numerical values of a patient's name were added to the day of the moon on which the man fell ill, and the prospects of his recovery could then be calculated.

What could have happened to Wiglaf on this mild spring day?

At last there was a step, and Wiglaf was back, smiling and closing the door with his strong, unwithered right arm. "Lord Redwald is back. I saw him, and he said he'd be here to see you before vespers." The dog went over to the fire and gave a crooked yawn.

"I sent you for some mistletoe and a cockerel, and you should have been able to accomplish all that without wasting a nobleman's patience." Still, Aethelwulf was pleased. It was always good to see Redwald. He had sensed that a special guest would arrive before nightfall; the cockerel would be a blessing.

Aethelwulf dried the mistletoe on the hearth, and then spread it on the table before him beside the white rooster. "Brother Aelle has been coughing, and a cough like that can disturb the sleep. Stir the fire, Wiglaf. We need some hot water. Tell me what I'm going to do."

"Why aren't you using mallow?"

"We're out of mallow."

"No, we have some still; let me—"

Aethelwulf tested a leaf in his fingers. "Mistletoe will help Brother Aelle sleep, and sleep is a great healer."

Redwald's bright red hair was always tousled, his cheeks ruddy, flushed with firelight or the wind. "My good friend," he said as he sat. "And good Wiglaf. I have come for a little of God's peace here."

"You can find such peace here, with masons' stone powder everywhere and Wiglaf teaching me how to be a physician?"

"I left the king's hall early. I heard something there that troubled my heart."

"What news disturbs a man-leader like yourself?" asked Aethelwulf.

"Don't you serve ale in this God haven?"

Wiglaf poured from the fine blue clay pitcher.

"There is something I want to ask you," said Redwald, his voice low, leaning forward so his shadow fell across the table. "I heard something in Eoforwic city that was always told to me with a whisper. No one can believe it. But it has everyone fighting phantoms in their sleep."

He glanced at Wiglaf as the youth ground the dry leaves. The old churchman gave a gesture—Wiglaf could be trusted.

"What," proceeded Redwald, "do holy men know that the rest of us have to discover?"

Aethelwulf bowed his head.

"Why haven't you told me?" Redwald asked.

Aethelwulf did not answer.

"This is my land, my people," said Redwald. "Every cowslip is dear to me—I am ring giver here. If there is any danger—"

"I know very little," said Aethelwulf, "but I'll tell you what I have heard." He clasped his hands, as if in prayer. And, indeed, he did pray for a moment.

Redwald waited.

"One night last summer ships of strange men streamed across the sea road out of the rising moon. They did not bother to comb downward along the coast. They knew they had no road enemy. They did not need to hide in the dark. They fell upon Lindisfarne, on the abbey there, and sacked it."

These words made Wiglaf stop his work, pestle heavy in his hand.

"Men died," Aethelwulf continued. "There was burning." Aethelwulf surprised himself. He wanted to weep. He was growing old. Or perhaps he could no longer think of human suffering. "And then they left with the gold from the altar. They didn't disturb Saint Cuthbert's bones. They slit only the throats of the living."

"Who were these brutes?"

"No one knows."

Redwald was a handsome man, Wiglaf thought, with a

sunrise-red beard, the only red-haired man Wiglaf had ever seen.

But the abbot saw quite a different guest from his open-eyed assistant. Redwald's habitual cheerfulness hid a nature given to nightmares—Redwald sometimes confessed them to the abbot. His fingernails were bitten to the quick, and weeks passed without Redwald being truly sober for more than a brief hour. Redwald's land extended along the river, all the way to Hunlaf's village, and south almost all the way to Bodeton, a town of fishers and boatbuilders, a worthless place despite its many dwellings. Lately Redwald had been spending his days drinking in the distant city of the king, or perhaps visiting the women who entertained men with fat purses.

"They won't come to our little place," said the abbot. "It was a punishment from God, no doubt for sins the monks had committed. We are in no danger. I didn't tell you because I knew you would tremble, and because it makes me sad to think of all the pain of that night. The strangers left to the east, and they haven't been seen since. If there were danger, it would have befallen us by now."

"Were the monks of that holy island unusually sinful?" asked Redwald.

Not even Brother Aelle dared ask the abbot such a straightforward question. Of course the monks of Lindisfarne were as chaste as most others and hardworking, by reputation. The abbot could not guess why they had been punished. "God looks upon the heart," said the priest.

"What sort of warriors," asked the nobleman after a long moment, "would do such harm to innocent men?"

"Don't ask questions I cannot begin to answer," said Aethelwulf.

"Summer's coming. Men sail when the sea is clear. It would be easy to sail the Humber and sweep up along our gentle river."

"I sleep easily," said Aethelwulf. He stretched a hand and patted Redwald's arm. "Lindisfarne is far from here. Look how bravely my student hears all this terrible news!"

Wiglaf was pleased that his eyes betrayed none of his feelings. He would dream that night of strangers, he was sure of it, and throats cut with flashing swords.

Redwald drank hard.

"If you spent more time in your spear hall, you would have heard of this before," the abbot chided gently.

Redwald gave a pained laugh. "I heard talk of this before, from Lord Hunlaf. He's a sightless old ring giver, but he hears everything. I chose not to heed."

"And is blind Hunlaf worried?" asked Aethelwulf. Hunlaf's upriver village was called Beckford, because a horseman could cross the river there during dry late summer weeks. The folk of Dunwic, however, called the place Hunlafwic, because the old man had been lord there for over forty years.

"Hunlaf says seafaring men would drown in our mud."

The abbot chuckled. "Hunlaf is a wise man."

"I'm off to the city again soon," said Redwald. "King Aethelred loves to meet at the ale table, full of plans for river wharves and well roofs."

"Enjoy the city, Redwald, and all its charms."

The nobleman gave the abbot a guarded glance. "My place is at the king's planning bench, good Father."

"Indeed it is. And we are safe."

Wiglaf crept over to Stag and stroked the dog. Stag was brave, Wiglaf knew, and would guard this holy place with his life.

"Safe, under Heaven's shield," said the abbot.

If only, thought Wiglaf, the good priest did not have that strained, uneasy note in his voice.

6

THE LATE AFTERNOON AIR was thick with smoke, the spice of manure, and the smell of wet thatch. The youth and the dog ran, Wiglaf avoiding puddles, the crook-jawed dog going out of his way to splash through them.

Wiglaf knew that he bothered Father Aethelwulf with his questions, but he wanted to know everything about medicine so that when he was old and wise, like the father, he would be a great healer. Medicine, Wiglaf had learned, was in the hands, but it was also in the voice. A hurt man who believed he would recover was stronger than a man sweaty with fear. Father Aethelwulf stewed alder leaves for the bowel flux, but offered it with a kind word, and advised what prayers to murmur.

Wiglaf knelt by Stag. *"Hwaet!"* he whispered. "Be still!"

Stag's crooked jaw made him look eternally happy, and perhaps he was. The little hamlet was quiet. Stonemasons muttered about the tethering in the crutch of a winch. One man swore by Saint Peter that it was tight enough, but another said he did not desire a mother stone intended for a corner of the tower to slip and make muck out of the limbs he had gotten up with that morning.

38

It was late in the day, but with the easing of winter and the longer hours of light, the men were still working in the fields or hammering in their shops, each man responsible for the mending of his own adze, each wife for her own brewing, each ox for his own digestion.

The sheep were in, the mud of the street unstirred by foot of man or beast. All the countryside was busy, except for Wiglaf. Wiglaf the tick. Wiglaf the bright-eyed, the spider. This was how he thought of himself. Wiglaf, the one who had to know and be alert and think, because he was not strong.

He was quick across the road, up to where the rolling cooking smoke flowed from the long white cottage with its peaked thatched roof.

He knelt in the doorway. He had street mud on his shoes, and he could not pretend to anyone that he was anywhere but where he was. Wiglaf made a whistle, sounding no note, only a long, thin wind.

A figure turned. The inside of the cot was smoke. It was always smoke, so that most people crept in the floor straw to avoid weeping because of the haze. The smoke found its way up out of a hole in the roof and out of the open, empty holes of the windows.

The figure rose through the smoke to the white rectangle of smoke around the door. Wiglaf held his breath. "I came to see you," he said before he knew who it was, and then a hand fell to his shoulder.

"Good Wiglaf, out of the books and into the mud," said Forni, one of the twins—his favorite brother, the one whose kicks had been mere jokes and had never hurt. "You've come back at a bad time to avoid a beating, Wig. Father is still furious about the bull, which has just now broken its tether. He's madder still that Lord Redwald spied the beast out in the water."

Wiglaf was pleased to hear Forni's voice.

"Mother's out there too. She heard Father bellowing. I've never seen him angrier, and if he sees you again today, he'll thump the brains right of here." Forni tapped Wiglaf's head with his finger.

"Mother's no doubt been mending rope," said Wiglaf.

"She does that while the dough swells. Check her window box."

Forni disappeared into the smoke, and then his silhouette eclipsed the distant window. The leather hinge of a chest creaked.

"Wiglaf the quick wit," said Forni, flourishing a rope. "Wiglaf the ever right. Wiglaf quicker than a flea. How did you know we had new rope hidden away?"

"Tie the bull with it," said Wiglaf. "Father will be pleased."

Their father entered the room, a grin cracking his muddy face. "I don't need this new handwork," he said. "I mended the old rope on the very spot, dear Forni. Between you and your brother, a goodwife could make brain mash enough for a finch. And you, my wandering cripple, my lord's gift to the house of God, what brings you to see me twice in one day?"

"Redwald and Aethelwulf have been sharing secrets," said Wiglaf.

His father found a three-legged stool and sat, his elbows on his knees.

"What sort of secrets, dear Wiglaf?" he asked.

There was no one more *hige-thitig*—stouthearted—

than his father, and perhaps his family would not need a warning after all. And besides, Wiglaf wondered, wasn't it wrong to repeat what he had heard at the churchman's table?

"Leave him." A broad woman swept by them. "Leave him; he's come to see us, and you needn't cause him hurt." She marched to the fire and stirred the soup—barley and turnip, judging by the smell—with a wooden paddle.

Wiglaf's father reached a hand and placed it on Wiglaf's head.

"Strangers burned a house of churchmen," said Wiglaf, "on the coast last year."

His father removed his hand from Wiglaf's head.

It was extremely bad luck to mention certain things, or to say certain words. No one ever spoke of Morcar, the eldest brother of Wiglaf and the twins. Morcar had broken a leg only last summer, striding home at dusk, his foot caving in a mole's tunnel, his shin giving like a rotted stick. His leg had turned the color of land, and his tongue had turned black. He had swollen like an oak gall and died. No one ever mentioned the walkers in the night, wood spirits and earth giants and the evil beings who killed travelers.

It was warm in the cot after the wind of the open field, and Wiglaf coughed. All of them busied themselves with opening a chest or tucking straw into place, preoccupied with Wiglaf's news, unsure how to respond.

Sigemund eyed his family: the two horselike twins and the bulk of a woman who had given him such pleasure and such day in–day out annoyance. And the little mouse of a lad—taller now, though, and quick-eyed. Not so much a mouse now, but something else. This was his family, and despite his hard nature he loved them. "I have heard," he said. "But I thought it was market gossip."

"The good abbot believes it's true," said Wiglaf. "Strangers burned the buildings and stole holy gold."

His father laughed. "Where did all this horror happen, Wiglaf?"

"At Lindisfarne."

"Where is that?"

"Off the coast," said Wiglaf, uttering words the meaning of which he did not entirely understand. He had never seen the coast, or the sea.

His father laughed. "That has nothing to do with us, lad."

Eadgifu poked the belly of the dough. It puckered like a navel, and then the dimple healed. She thanked Saint Giles that her husband had not struck dear Wiglaf. It had made her sick in her bones when he struck her youngest son all those years. When Lord Redwald had taken Wiglaf away, it had been a golden day. She had wept with happiness. She missed Wiglaf. Anyone would miss the boy—he was like a summer morning—but he was safe, and only a walk across the road and down a field would bring him here for a wedge of bread.

Sigemund drank deeply from his ale cup. "You get filled with words and pictures sitting around listening to a churchman," said Wiglaf's father. "Father Aethelwulf has a good heart, but little field sense. And Lord Redwald is well enough, in his way, but what do these men know about a strong arm and a hungry ax?"

The twins left to call the cows. Their falsettos reached through the walls, almost like song.

"We have many stonemasons here in the village," said Sigemund.

Wiglaf's mother knew that a dozen stoneworkers lived in the spear hall, and all of them were from far away, up the river from the city, or even beyond that. They had strange accents. Who knew what harm might come from the evil-eye glance of a strange man upon a pregnant woman? Still, they added strength to the small collection of villagers.

"Those stories of terrible things in faraway places should not worry your mother. Look at her—already afraid! Don't give Wiglaf's stories a thought, wife. He's been listening to church prattle."

New things were rare and unimportant. What was handed down, from mother to daughter to daughter, achieved value by all the lives it spoke for. Eadgifu had a precious jet brooch she kept in a birch-wood chest in the corner. It was the sole treasure this peasant family had worth stealing.

Wiglaf's mother knew all the charms by heart. She knew the magic to keep a bee swarm from traveling far (*Take earth, cast it with your right hand and say . . .*) and she knew land remedies, both the one for pasture-land and the one for plough land. She knew the charms for winning a lover, how to think of your beloved as you uncovered the moon before your eyes and hope that you dreamed of him that night.

But in the face of disturbing tidings from far away, there were only the saints to seek for help. She said that Heaven would protect them from the Devil and from blood-lusting strangers.

"Of course Heaven will," said Wiglaf's father.

"Don't you think a stoneworker would be like stone?" said Wiglaf's mother, smiling at Wiglaf.

"Unforgiving?" offered Wiglaf.

"No, that's not what I mean. Strong."

"So a man who herds sheep would be sheeplike," joked Wiglaf.

"And a man who lives in a monastery would turn dark and damp," said Wiglaf's father. This playful speech was a favorite game among the folk of Dunwic, each one trying to outdo the other. Wiglaf believed his father, for all his roughness, was nearly as shrewd as Father Aethelwulf, though not half as wise or merciful.

His father began telling the old story of the dragon that lived in an *aldwark,* an ancient stone ruin, and how a man from Dunwic had killed the fiery beast with a wood ax. "Cut him head and spine," said Sigemund, lifting his own ax from its place against the wall and letting the firelight play along its edge. "And so I'll cleave the head of any stranger," he added, showing his yellow teeth. "I wish they would come soon."

1

AETHELWULF AND REDWALD still sat in the light
from a beeswax candle when Wiglaf returned that
evening. The scent of the honey wax and the light were
precious to Aethelwulf, like the love he felt for his Savior.

Redwald and Aethelwulf ate the roast cockerel and
drank brown ale. They drank mead, and they drank from
a silver pitcher of Rhône wine. Redwald enjoyed speech
sport as much as any man in Dunwic, and he asked
Wiglaf if the lad had heard any new riddles.

"One or two, my lord." It was both polite and wise to
wait for a ring giver like Redwald to offer permission, especially when one was seeking to baffle him in a game.

"Go on," urged Redwald.

"*I am cut, polished, stirred, dried, bleached, soft-
ened—*"

"Too easy, Wiglaf. The answer is ale."

"You tell one, then," prompted the abbot.

"I believe I shall. A crafty one indeed. *My nose is
downward. As I travel on one side, all is grassy; on the
other track, gleaming black—*"

"A riddle fit for a child," laughed Aethelwulf. "A plow.
Everyone knows that."

Wiglaf said that he knew yet another, one Brother Aelle had told him.

"Brother Aelle knows a riddle?" said Aethelwulf.

"*A foe stole my life. He dipped me in hot sun where I shed my hair. A bird's joy and power sprinkled me over with meaningful drops. It made frequent tracks with its swallowed tree dye—*"

Redwald lifted a hand in mock surrender. "A monkish riddle, and I'll never guess it."

"A book, my lord!" said Wiglaf.

Redwald laughed, and then said, "But I know nothing of books. They are always in Latin, every verse, and I have a head only for the English tongue, which only a monk would ever write down."

Wiglaf listened in fascination as the two men began gossiping about the women of Fulford, a town of lascivious female folk, shameless as mares in heat, just outside the big city itself. "Pray for the souls of these women," said Redwald. "And for the souls of the poor sinners who have to pass by their village on the way to see the king."

Aethelwulf did not like to hear of such sinful bed play. And yet it did have a certain curious wonderment to it, an entire village of such fallen beauties. "And you have to ride through this town, my good Lord Redwald—there is no other route?"

"I ride north again in a day or two, back to another hall counsel, and my path will take me straight through this town of dazzling sinners."

"How terrible for you," said Aethelwulf.

"It is a strain, good Father," he agreed, with a wry smile. "A challenge indeed."

But both of them knew there were dangers in the wild spaces, descendants of Cain or children of Hell. This was why timber-stout walls were built, and why good men and women lived together. The threat of sinful women was a trifling matter.

"When I was young I used to converse with Alcuin the great scholar," said Aethelwulf. "I had much to un-learn. I was as lusty as any hay cutter during the long summer twilights. I thought that dipping my goose-quill pen in oak-gall ink would cure me of lust, spending long hours writing holy texts."

"And did it?"

Rain breathed against the shuttered window. The candle flame shivered. Aethelwulf gathered his robe around him. "Lust is a sin, Redwald," he said. "But the greatest sin is not to trust God."

"Indeed, I put my faith in Heaven," said the nobleman.

"When you see the king again—" Aethelwulf was about to say, *Ask for shields and spears and helmets. Ask for chain mail and sword gloves.* But instead he said, "Give him my blessing."

The abbot saw the drink-sodden Redwald onto his horse, Wiglaf helping the nobleman into the saddle. The lord's hall was a not a long ride through the night, and Redwald had been known to drink a goatskin of red wine at one sitting, and then ride all night to the king's table.

"I'll tell of the church tower, how it rises skyward," said Redwald, gesturing into the dark. "In the great city walls I sing of the glory of Dunwic," he half chanted, sounding like a tale sayer. Redwald was very drunk in-deed. His horse splashed off into the darkness.

"Wiglaf, you will show me to my bed," said the old priest. "My eyes are not as keen in darkness as they used to be. And I am weary from a day of study."

"And perhaps, Father, the Rhône wine argued with the ale in your belly," said Wiglaf with a certain politeness.

"A physician should learn of such things," said Aethelwulf.

The abbot woke in the night and without wondering why, groped for his staff. There was no reason to expect it beside his bed. But when he could not find it he sat up and crept toward the wall to the place where it was leaning.

Such a terrible dream! Aethelwulf struck the span of ash wood on the stone floor. The staff made a ringing whisper.

He was a man of God, but in his youth he had handled an ax with skill. He stood in the darkness, holding his staff like a weapon. Could I now, wondered the priest, lift my arm and strike a man, knock him to the ground?

Could I fight hard enough to save the lives of the people I love?

8

WIGLAF READ IN A CLEAR, CAREFUL VOICE.

Aethelwulf had never been a compassionate person in his early years but now, after decades of study and effort, he had become exactly what he had hoped to be: loving, and at peace. Saint Benedict had taught that to work was to pray. Now Aethelwulf believed that on some blessed days, to breathe was to pray.

Wiglaf was struggling through the lives of the saints. This was a precious book, one of the most holy in the abbey. The boy read of Erkengota, a saint whose corpse had exuded a balsamlike odor. He read of Dismas, the good thief, who died with Our Lord. And he read of Giles, the patron saint of cripples. That holy man had lived in solitude in a forest, and had been wounded by an arrow intended for a hind.

The boy stumbled on a word. *"Excepit,"* said Aethelwulf. *"Excipere*—you remember, surely."

"'Capture,'" said Wiglaf.

"Very good. 'To capture.' And that's *ferum,* 'wild animal.' They are hunting the wild deer, the hind, with a *saevo cane*—a fierce dog." He gave a quiet laugh. "Perhaps it's as fierce as Stag."

Wiglaf could learn as quickly as Aethelwulf could teach. It was a challenge, and Aethelwulf relished it. In his old age he had discovered this joy. As the boy read the handsome Latin sentences, the storied archer raised his weapon.

The arrow left the ignorant hunter's bow and pierced the saint.

Latin was the prince of all languages, but the next dawn Aethelwulf did something he had never done before. He began a poem—verses that the men and women of his parish would be able to understand. It was in their own earthy language, the speech of husbands and wives and horsemen. He marveled as he worked the poem in his mind what a fit word for God it was, and how God's power broke through the sounds of the syllables like light through a cloud. "*Micel,*" he said to himself. "Great. The Great God."

He did not write down this poem with a quill and ink. Perhaps someday in the future he would have one of the brothers commit it to one of the vellum rolls that were not of the best quality. He kept the poem in his mind where he could knead it, where, with time, he believed it would grow golden and, if it were not too much to hope for, glorious.

Frea, the wife of Alfred, sent for help. One of her children, afraid to look around at this room of books and beeswax candles, asked for the good father's attention. "She can't get out of bed," said the short, round-headed peasant boy in the accent of field folk.

Wiglaf and the abbot set off together.

The clay cutter was a moderately wealthy peasant, the descendant of generations of men with skill in preparing the earth used in building walls. The problem with Frea, as far as Wiglaf knew, was that she was the most grumpy woman in the world. She was meaner than a gander, thought Wiglaf, walking, as was proper, a full stride behind the abbot. Frea would argue with a stump.

"Frea has rheumatism," said Aethelwulf, perhaps reading Wiglaf's mind. His mother had said that some wise folk had such thought-stealing power, and it would not surprise Wiglaf if the abbot was one of them. "We must have sympathy for her."

"She's the greatest scold," Wiglaf offered, feeling immediately ashamed of himself.

The abbot did not respond to this remark. "There is more nonsense about rheumatism than any other ailment. Some people think that if you drink the water a fox has been boiled in you can cure it. The truth is, Wiglaf, nothing can cure it."

Aethelwulf put on his most cheerful manner as he entered the cot. To Wiglaf's surprise, it worked.

"I've never been strong," Frea said gently, without a trace of her usual humor. "Always given over to a fever every now and then."

"It's not easy. Heaven understands this."

"But you're so happy, Father. Happy Father I call you. Nothing ever troubles you."

Perhaps the abbot laughed too loudly. Frea's head fell back to her rush-stuffed pillow-sack. "I shouldn't have spoken so, good Father. Please forgive me."

"No, it pleases me to hear it," said Aethelwulf. "As a

younger man, and not so long ago as a not-young man, people thought me a very sour person. Always bitter, thinking how things could be and how they never were what they ought to be. With reason, I suppose—things never are quite what we hope. But something has happened to me since I came here to Dunwic. I've become happy. We don't have to be happy to be a child of God, you know. There's no reason to expect joy."

Aethelwulf advised Frea to drink warm water. "Not after a fox has been cooked in it, or drunk from it, or anything at all having to do with a fox."

On their way back to the abbey, Wiglaf said that Frea looked different.

"She has something very wrong with her, Wiglaf," said Aethelwulf. "You saw her eyes?"

"The whites were yellow."

"What does that mean to you?"

Wiglaf considered. He already knew that Aethelwulf now believed that Frea was a very sick woman. But what was the ailment called, and what prayer or what herb could cure it? Wiglaf admitted he did not know.

"I don't know either," said Aethelwulf. "Perhaps she wants to have some peace in her last days. It takes so much courage, Wiglaf, just to be an ordinary man or woman."

9

THE SEA CRASHED AROUND *RAVEN*.

Lidsmod shivered, soaked to the skin through his tunic.

The heavy salt water drenched the wool clothing, and the rough salty fabric chafed the flesh. Lidsmod was bailing, flinging water over the side.

Ulf took the bailer when Lidsmod had to pause, out of breath. The big bald-headed man flung brine into the wind, although most of it streamed back into his face, and dripped from his beard. The bailer was oak, half bucket and half shovel. When Ulf was red-faced and panting, Trygg, a man whose nose had been nearly cut off in a fight out of legend, took over, and when Trygg wearied, something happened that stirred the men of *Raven* with surprise.

Torsten, the berserker, took the bailer, drew a deep breath, and when he was finished, there was no water in the ship. He handed the bailer to Opir, who wore it on his head for a while.

"What it takes for the sea," Njord said to Lidsmod, "is not courage, or bear spirit, or anything like that. You want to be a steady man—*hofsmadr*. Someone your mates can depend on, the way they can depend on this steering oar." Some day, Njord had promised, Lidsmod could be a helmsman, someone the ship would trust. But this was not likely to be any time soon, Lidsmod believed. Njord handed Lidsmod a dried, tough stick of salted herring, and the two of them drank a few swallows of morning ale, just enough to take the bite out of the salt spray.

Njord gripped the tiller in his right hand. He looked upward at the sky, as though he were not sailing the ocean at all, but the heavens. Lidsmod sat beside him on the raised platform beside the steering oar. This far at sea they had a good following wind, and no oars had to be manned.

"Feel how *Raven* flexes with the swells," said Njord. The red-striped sail blossomed. *Raven* seemed to leave the water. She rarely rocked from side to side, like a freight *knorr,* but always upward, flexing like a living creature, so that the ship seemed to climb the sky.

Raven was a good name for a first voyage, but a truly fortunate ship would earn a better, longer, or more storied name. *Crane,* while a fine vessel, had never become *Crane of the Wind,* or *Crane of the Victories,* because something about the ship had seemed not quite saga fit. *Landwaster,* on the other hand, had once been called simply *Fulmar,* after the strong-winged seabird.

A petrel scurried across the water, heading north-northwest. *Raven* coursed toward the southwest. Now that the oars were stowed, the sail billowed, and the walrus-hide stays fastened, the men occupied themselves by doing little: drowsing, talking quietly, enduring the water and the cold.

54

Njord reached up and tested the tension of the back stay. *Raven* was so flexible that even this tug could be felt throughout the ship. "Climb forward to the bowline," Njord told Lidsmod. "Make sure it's taut."

Lidsmod scrambled over sea chests and lounging bodies. The bowline was fastened at the base of *Raven's* prow. Lidsmod tugged at the rope, and a yellow grin appeared at his shoulder. "Don't pull it like that—you'll snap it in two." Gorm shoved Lidsmod aside. "Many a good line's been broken by a clumsy hand."

Lidsmod said, "Njord wants it tighter."

"He wants it tighter," scoffed Gorm. "Njord knows everything about a ship, doesn't he? So if Njord wants a tighter line, that is exactly what Njord will get."

Gorm's words were fit enough, but his manner turned something in Lidsmod's heart.

"We tighten it like this." Gorm stretched the line, untied and retied the knot in the space of three breaths. It was an expert knot, quickly executed. "Tighten the tack line on your way back," Gorm said with a tight-lipped smile.

The tack was fastened through an oar hole, and at first it looked easier than the bowline had. But the hide rope was stiff, and Lidsmod's fingers were clumsy with the cold and wet. Lidsmod stepped on a hand, and Eirik's eye opened.

"There's nothing wrong with that knot, friend Lidsmod," said the saga teller sleepily. "Leave it alone."

It was too late. Three things happened at once.

Njord called out, "What are you doing?"

The tack line popped out of the oar hole and whipped into the wind.

And Gorm laughed.

The ship faltered, the sail flapping like a great white blood-splashed wing. The tack line slashed Lidsmod on the mouth, and his hands could not grab it as it blinked past him again.

Ulf bulked close to Lidsmod and soothed the sail down. Eirik stood and reached out to the canvas, gathering in the snaking line.

"That happens to everyone who ever sailed," said Ulf reassuringly. "A man can stand all morning trying to snatch a loose line from the wind. Loop it through the oar hole and use a surf knot. Tug it tight. That's all you have to do."

It hadn't needed to be done at all, Lidsmod realized. Eirik had been right. Lidsmod was flushed with humiliation and stumbled over sea chests and huddled bodies, back toward the helm. He stared into the wind so that the hard breeze would seem to have caused his tears.

"Grab the bailer," Njord ordered, matter-of-fact. "Get that water over the side."

Lidsmod bailed. He had bailed since his infancy, as had any boy, in skips, small shore boats, with his friends. He could do it at least as well as most of the men, and even better, if he worked hard at it, than Torsten the berserker. He knew how to fling the water so it vanished into the wind, and he was quick.

Gorm steamed inwardly, keeping his own counsel.

Was there no other way to gain gold in the world than to endure these clumsy dimwits? he thought. Every one of them was stupid in some way. Torsten, with his bear shirt and his dull eye, who had to concentrate to swallow his spit so he didn't drool. Floki, with his slick, smug expression, because he had won Gorm's thirty sheep. Njord with his skull-cracked glee in the ocean, like a little boy in a fishing cog. And Gunnar with his pretense of not hearing what was said around him.

Gorm said nothing. It was important to endure these men, because he needed gold more than ever. Gorm bit his lip and turned away. The sea rose up; the sea fell away. It did not interest Gorm.

"This is a good wind," Njord said, explaining why wet and chill were good things, blessings from Odin. Lidsmod was willing to believe it, and was thankful he wasn't seasick. That would have been deep humiliation indeed. But already his old neighbors from the village looked different; the cold made the men look gaunt and unfamiliar. Even Gunnar looked cruel and watchful, and the poet Eirik drowsed sullenly, arms folded against the salt spumes.

But the ship's weather vane was, indeed, stretched straight as a black knife. "Three days and we'll kiss land," said Njord.

Lidsmod allowed himself to feel a flicker of optimism. "We'll surprise the Westland, like snow out of a summer sky," he said, using the old saying hopefully. "Especially with a berserker like Torsten."

"Give me men like Trygg," Njord confided quietly, "with his beak like two noses where a Dane sliced it. He's left-handed as well as even-tempered. Sometimes a left-handed man has an advantage in a battle. Men like Ulf are good shipmates too, and Eirik, whose mood is steady and whose poetry can ease even death. But a berserker . . ." Njord could not bring himself to say more.

Gunnar stirred. The wind freshened, so he sent men to shorten the sail. But if Gunnar had said nothing, the work would have been done soon enough. These men needed no sea lord.

"I knew this ship would fly!" cried Njord. He had augered the holes and driven the pegs. The steering oar, a broad wooden paddle fastened to the side of the ship, was held like a large sword into the water. It was always on the right side of the ship, the steer-board side. The oar sliced the water cleanly. Njord told Lidsmod that the feel of it in his hands was the best feeling in the world.

The blue-black waves fell away. White foam skeined the face of the water. The timbers and the rigging groaned like great god-women under the thrusts of god-men. Njord spat salt water. The wool sail did not flap or billow. It stayed hard, pregnant-woman full. "Maybe two days," said Njord, "at this speed."

Lidsmod glanced back. *Crane* was keeping up, he'd give it that. At this distance it was a twin to *Raven,* but Lidsmod knew that *Crane* could not beat against the wind, if it came to that, like this new *Raven* could.

Landwaster was far behind, a black gnat on the water. But it did not have to be fast. Five hundred men had died because of that ship, and the five hundred Danish death agonies seemed to weigh it down. It was an ugly ship, and nearly crank, tending to lean sideways into the water.

A wave ran under *Raven,* pattering underfoot like mice, rolling forward. The stern lifted with the overtaking wave, and the prow nodded. Now not only the wind was pushing *Raven,* but the sea too, blue cliffs rising behind them, urging them forward.

That night, the invisible spray stinging lips and eyes, Eirik sang. His song was of the broad loom of slaughter, the human web. The Fates crossed it with a scarlet weft, and the warp was made of human entrails. Human heads were the loom weights.

Lidsmod wished Eirik had sung another tale. Ulf, however, grunted with satisfaction when the saga was done. Like most of the men, he took solace from these cold stories, cold and true. Such stories helped a man endure real weather. There was solace for the fallen, but first they had to fall.

The men ate salt herring. Eirik sang another song, and this one Lidsmod liked. It was the *Saga of Landwaster*. The ship fell from the north, and the Danes in their mead halls did not know it had gathered them until the oak halls burned. They ran, sword in hand, through the death gates, and the men of *Landwaster*, the sons of Spjothof, cut them one by one to the bone. Then came the counterattack, the attack of the wolf king, lord of the Danes, failing badly, and the surf splashing thick with the blood of the spearmen, the Danes all killed.

Give me men to kill, thought Gorm, listening to the tale. He would have prayed to the One-eyed, but Gorm had no god. For him there was nothing beyond this world of black sea, black sky. But still he thought, Give me men to kill. He hungered for a circle of death around him.

When every man was asleep or trying to sleep in the cold and wet, and Ulf was at the helm, the sky changed. The stars dimmed and vanished. The wind slackened.

No one had to wake the men. They stirred, dim

shapes in the dark. The sail was lowered, furled around the yard, and lashed to its supports. Men wrapped sea blankets around their shoulders, and Njord took the steering oar. He gripped it with both hands. It was not surprising this time of year, a storm out of the east. Now they would see how strong *Raven* was.

Lidsmod knew not to ask. He scowled the same way Torsten scowled, and Trygg, because it was essential to have a manly look on his face. But soon he slipped to the helm and whispered to Njord, "What will happen?"

The white-haired helmsman chuckled. "We'll see what our fine *Raven* can do in a storm!"

L IDSMOD HAD NEVER BEEN SO AFRAID.

Raven went under again, and then bounded into the air. Beards streamed water. Men hung on to sea chests. Lidsmod took his turn with the bailing scoop, and then clung to the side of the ship, half blind with flying spray.

Trygg, his scarred nose streaming brine, bailed. It did no good. Eirik took another bailer and shoveled water too. No one spoke. It would have been useless. The wind raked the ship. Lidsmod tried to take heart in the knowledge that every man had experienced this before—some of them had been in ships that had capsized in storms, or in ships that had burst like rush baskets against rocks. The men held on, eyes tight against the sting of salt water.

Opir hooted once when *Raven* stood nearly on end and then fell back. But now Opir was quiet too.

Ulf checked the line around Lidsmod's waist. He put his face against Lidsmod's ear. "Don't worry!" he called. "*Raven* will play with the wind!"

To trust in the ship was to trust in the ship's ancestors, in the pine for the mast and the oars, and the oaks that stood into the storms as they grew. It was to trust in earth and rain. The powers of the sky were in *Raven* as she shouldered upward from the sea.

Raven plunged back, but the waves had fallen away, so that she fell farther, down so far that Lidsmod could see the cliffs of water high around her. Water swallowed ship and crew. Through the dark they ascended, higher and yet higher, beyond what had been the surface of the waves. And still higher yet. The sky was made of water now. The earth was gone.

Lidsmod had seen a god once. This was not something he would tell just anyone—when a god showed himself, it was not a secret you always shared with other men. Climbing into the highlands to carry a cheese to his uncle, who had scruffy sheep up where it was always winter, Lidsmod had seen a man standing at the crossing of two trails, a one-eyed man who did not speak but only watched. When the youth lifted a hand in greeting, this figure lifted his, in turn. Lidsmod stood in the path and waited as the unfamiliar man climbed the hill path and vanished.

He mentioned this to his mother one night beside the fire; she did not answer for a long time. When she finally spoke, she said that Odin might take something from Lidsmod—a finger, or perhaps an entire limb. "This will be his way of keeping you safe, and accepting a fee in turn." She said this without joy, and Lidsmod regretted telling her about the gnarled traveler by the stony path.

Maybe now, thought Lidsmod, is when Odin will crush a thumb, or blind one of my eyes. He tried to stay close to Ulf, because the broad-shouldered man was known to be good luck—years ago Ulf's grandfather had caught a dwarf.

This was a famous incident, and everyone knew about it. Dwarves could make marvelous things of gold. They were cunning with their hands, and if a man waited near the earth cracks where they lived, and caught one in a net, he could make the dwarf carve or mold something for him before he was let go. Dwarves live in the ground like elves, and are notoriously cautious. Ulf's grandfather had been a clear-headed freeman, widely known for his intelligence. He trapped the dwarf on Midsummer night, when there was no darkness at all, so that the dwarf was overconfident. Odin loves the sly.

The dwarf, snagged and bound, agreed to make a cloak pin of gold; this was the brooch Ulf's father wore on feasting days. It was a simple piece, and not as intricate as much dwarf work, but it was heavy with its richness, being pure gold, with a copper pin. Ulf's brother would inherit it, and this was all the gold Ulf's family had. He had a proud family, much admired, and they worked hard and feared no man.

Even to run a farm a man needed slaves, but who in Spjothof could afford such people? The folk of the village were warriors, and proud. No one would laugh in the port halls of the north if a man said he was from Spjothof. It was a village that carried its name well. But it did take slaves to work a farm properly. Three slaves for a farm of twelve cows and two horses—this was what a man needed. But no one in Spjothof had the gold to buy slaves from the Swedish traders, and no one in Spjothof would suffer a Dane for a slave.

Without gold, how could a man pay bride-price? And without bride-price, there would be no bridal ale. A three-year ox would not be slaughtered. There would be no feast. There would be no wife. Gold was the cure to all the ills of every man in *Raven*. Every shipmate sailed in an attempt to solve the problem of poverty or the curse of being the youngest son.

Lidsmod huddled. He coughed water. The inside of his nose burned with salt. He did not know if he huddled against the planks, or against Ulf's sea chest, or against Trygg's leather sole. He did all of that at once, flung from bottom to side to foot, and back again. He was soaked and icy cold. His fingers were wrinkled. He kept himself rolled like a sea snail, so that he would not bump his head.

This was not a storm, thought Lidsmod. A storm was waves and wind and rain, perhaps even lightning. No, this was the constant sinking of a ship. *Raven* plunged into the wall of water. The men were all underwater, their shoulders hunched. Then the ship was in the sky. It was out of the water entirely, a thrown spear.

Lidsmod was not afraid of drowning. He had something more important to fear. He was going to vomit! These warriors would never be seasick. They had all been through worse. This was probably not a storm to them at all, Lidsmod felt. They were probably asleep, most of them, bored by what was to them slightly choppy water.

Njord wrestled with the steering oar. His face streamed water so that it seemed the beardless white-haired man had a long beard of sea. He blew sea from his mouth. And he looked joyous! Lidsmod wondered if his good friend was suddenly mad. Of course, Lidsmod reminded himself, a salty helmsman like Njord would love a storm like this.

And Lidsmod was about to throw up. He had been on boats since he was an infant, but never a great ship like this, and never in a storm. Lidsmod clenched his fists. He would not be sick! He willed it. I, Lidsmod, he thought, son of Leif and Fastivi, sharer of the *Raven*'s glory, will not be sick. I will not vomit. I will not bring shame to myself and to my mother.

The plank at his nose had a golden pattern. The details of the wood, the little blond currents of it, were composed, he saw for the first time, of even slighter details, like the hairs of a golden woman. Like the secret hair of Hallgerd, the jarl's daughter, tall and high-breasted, that night under the last fat moon of spring. Lidsmod tried to fight off his nausea by recalling vividly that one coupling, his only such experience, at the edge of the sheep meadow.

When all the young women threw spears in a yearly contest after the harvest, Hallgerd's went farthest, buried deep in the green earth. Why was it that such a gifted young woman would take Lidsmod in, and lie quietly with him afterward, listening to promises of bride-price, of a future home with a fine birch-and-poplar loom?

Raven fell, and this time the ship descended forever. Ropes rose into the air, and drops lifted like snow and stood suspended. Men floated, their bodies light, even weightless, as *Raven* found the hole through the earth and fell. It was not falling. It was downward flight.

And then it was not downward. *Raven* was suspended in midflight.

Without seeming to touch water, the ship flexed, arched like a seal, and began to ascend. *Raven* climbed fast. Men were flattened to the planks, feeling two or three times their normal weight. The water in the hull was flat and leaden, and even the air was heavy, scooped into the ship.

Like a man walking at the bottom of the sea, Trygg stood up, swayed to the side, and let out a terrible sound. What sort of coughing curse speech was that? Lidsmod wondered. And then he knew.

Trygg had vomited! Trygg Two-nose, a man out of song, a warrior whose strength was doubted by no one, had vomited over the side of the ship! Lidsmod was deeply relieved. There would be no shame upon his mother. There would be no humiliation upon Lidsmod's long-dead father. If Trygg had to vomit, then anyone could.

But Lidsmod was not sick. The wind tired, as quickly as it took to be aware of it. The waves shook and threatened on all sides, like a struggling crowd, but the new silence stunned Lidsmod.

Men stood and blinked up at the sky. They searched the ocean around them. Far off, *Crane* took a wave peak and then slid easily down a slope of sea. Sunlight spilled onto the ocean. The sound of Ulf's bailing was loud, a splashing, grunting struggle with water. Opir the boaster, silent now, took the bailer from Ulf, and Floki took the other one.

Landwaster was nowhere. It could not be seen.

The men could not say the name of the dark ship. To talk about it would be a mistake—to mention a possible misfortune practically guaranteed it would take place. But every man looked back, again and then again. The sea was busy, like an army of gray shields. But it was true—*Landwaster* was gone.

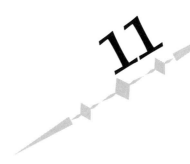

LIDSMOD GAZED BACK, until he told himself it would do no good to worry. Either the ship was afloat or it was not. Nevertheless it would be very bad if *Landwaster* was gone. All the men they had known since childhood, all the blood brothers and cousins—Lidsmod could not think about such a bitter loss.

Gunnar would not meet the eyes of his men. He knew they were looking at him for a clue as to how they should feel. Calm? Worried? Should they turn back and search? A mark appeared on Gunnar's cheek, a scar that showed only on rare occasions. As a youth, the story went, Gunnar had slipped on the first ice of autumn and cut himself on the head of a harpoon he'd won in a wrestling match. Lidsmod knew that if *Landwaster* had capsized, every man was gone. There was a song about a man saved by a large seal on a stormy night, and Lidsmod had half believed a man could be saved that way.

But this cold morning was real—it was not a song.

"Lidsmod," said Gunnar at last. "Climb to the top of the mast."

He did not hesitate, not with every man watching. He climbed. One side of the mast was already dry from the wind; the other was icy wet. His legs and arms wrapped the pine mast and were nearly not strong enough for the task. Until he was about the height of the tallest of them, the robust Ulf, it would simply be a struggle to climb at all. The weather vane twitched and fluttered high above.

The very top of the mast was too far away. But Lidsmod struggled upward, the mast pressed against his ribs, his legs wrapped around it. Every man on *Raven* was either watching, or watching with his thoughts. Gradually the mast tapered, and it was easier to get a grip.

But now the mast pitched and shivered. The ship wobbled far below, and Lidsmod gasped at how strange it looked, how crowded with men, and how small. It was a fifteen bencher, and not as big as some ships. But from this height it looked too frail to protect thirty and more human beings.

Don't look down, thought Lidsmod. Don't look anywhere. Just hang on. Close your eyes and climb and ignore the cold and the drunken stagger of the ship.

The ship fought and dodged. The weather vane snapped just above Lidsmod, then just at his ear. This was the very end of the mast, and he opened his eyes.

He slipped.

He closed his eyes and hung on tight. He imagined hearing the even voice of his mother, the tone she used when a fishing boat was late during a squall, saying that their faith would balance the harm and keep it from happening. He pictured Hallgerd's gray eyes, believing Lidsmod when he said that some day he would bring gold and glory to the table of her father.

Climb again, he told himself, and he did, very slowly, until once again the salt-stiff weather vane was at his ear.

He glanced down.

A mistake. Opir's pale face gazed upward, his smile offering silent encouragement. Opir's father had failed to wake one morning last summer and had gradually drifted away into a deeper and deeper sleep, until he stopped breathing altogether. Opir had been all the more reckless ever since, his voice louder than before, but Lidsmod guessed that of all his shipmates Opir was the one who knew sorrow and anxiety best.

At a word from Njord, Opir looked away, fussing with a knot. To show support for the young man's effort, each shipmate pretended to ignore Lidsmod, every man a study in preoccupation. Lidsmod hung on in wind that was cold and strong and swept his hair back and filled his eyes with tears. He couldn't see if he looked into the wind, and he couldn't see if he looked away from it. The mast tossed.

Water stretched to the horizon, its surface gleaming copper and silver with the sunlight. There was *Crane,* skimming the waves, spearing them.

No sign of *Landwaster.*

12

IT WAS A LONG NIGHT.

Crane stayed so close to *Raven* that Lidsmod could hear the voices of men across the water. They did not speak often, though—words were powerless. What could Odin give them in exchange for the loss of these men, and this famous ship?

Eirik told the song of the Last Battle, when the gods themselves would bleed. Nothing escaped. Even the immortals suffered.

Njord would not let Gunnar take the helm, nor Ulf, who was an able steersman. It would not be right for him to abandon his place at a time like this. Every man should do exactly what he did best. That, Njord explained to Lidsmod, was one good way to help the Regin, the deciding powers of the universe, spare lives. If each man did what was proper, and followed his skill, it was possible that all would be well.

All night the ship creaked and the water rolled under the keel. The Norns could not be beaten. But sometimes—almost never, but sometimes—they grew inattentive.

In first light Gunnar had the sail lowered and told Lidsmod to climb the mast again.

Men paid no notice. What Gunnar did, and what Lidsmod did in turn, could not be acknowledged. Eirik mended a rope. Trygg honed a knife with a black stone. Opir worked a new leather thong through the seam in his shoe.

It was easier now. Lidsmod's arms and legs were sore from the first climb, but he knew he could do it, and the sea was calm. It rose and it fell easily, like a horse's breathing. When he reached the mast top, the weather vane was slack. It twitched, fell, and lifted restlessly.

The sea was like a vast glacier, wrinkled, dead. *Crane* parted the water, leaving a slick wake. A gull, hungry for fish scraps, gazed at Lidsmod from just out of reach. Its yellow beak was bright, and its black eye was tiny and knew exactly what it was doing, studying this ship full of men.

Gray water. Nothing more.

Lidsmod clung to the mast, searching the horizon. He should climb down soon, he knew, before the cold worked into his sinews.

Then: something.

At the very end of the sea, as far away as Lidsmod could perceive, a shape like a sheep fly. It was there for half a breath, and then it was gone.

"What do you see?" said Gunnar. His voice was far away, from another world.

Lidsmod held tight and looked down. He gave a doubtful look: he didn't know.

Trygg slapped the mast with his big hand, and Lidsmod could feel his strength all the way to the top. Trygg couldn't bear it—what did Lidsmod see?

The fly lifted and fell. Lidsmod blinked, trying to clear his eyes.

Nothing. And then there was something again, a fleck, a dark shape. The ship—because it was a ship— had a white sail with red stripes. The sun caught the sail.

"I see them!" cried Lidsmod. "I see *Landwaster!*"

It was important to use the right speech, the right tone of voice. Gunnar called upward. "Are you sure?"

Was Lidsmod sure? He strained. Red stripes. A black ship, winking in and out of the distant sea.

He spoke clearly, sounding, he hoped, like a seasoned seafarer. "To the north, in a line off the helm. *Landwaster!*"

Men slapped him on the back when he was down from the mast, and Opir called him Lidsmod the ship spier, the man with eyes nearly as keen as Trygg's— Trygg, the man who could count the wrinkles on a whale.

Landwaster came up slowly. Gunnar called out, asking what was wrong, and the answer came back, a voice in the wind, that nothing indeed was wrong, and why were *Crane* and *Raven* so far off course?

It had taken them a day and a night to find them, said Egil from *Landwaster,* his voice tiny in the wind, but sharp too, hoarse with the cold.

Men laughed and groaned. Even Torsten smiled, and it had been a long time since the berserker had shown happiness.

"Thank you for rescuing us!" called Opir.

A shearwater played across the waves. It was a land bird that flew well over water, and usually alone. Njord showed Lidsmod how to read the horizon, what clouds were sea clouds, which might be land mist. Lidsmod could smell it. They all could.

No one spoke. Every movement was tense, deliberate. The golden time, the day they had lived for during the long winter, might be taken from them by the immortals at this last moment.

Njord squinted. "Almost a sad sight," he said ironically. "I wish we could keep sailing to the edge of the world."

"No gold at the edge of the earth," said Opir. "Only giants to squash crazy helmsmen." His voice was higher pitched than usual.

Gorm smiled, panting openmouthed like a wolf.

Eirik sang a song softly, mostly to himself. It was about a magic ring that made its wearer invisible. It was about a traveler who, while invisible, could steal gold from sleeping dragons.

Gorm thought of gold and fire: let a Westland dweller or two try to stop me from gathering the treasures. Let them try, he thought. He looked forward to killing as much as he looked forward to gold.

Lidsmod wished he could be more sure of what lay ahead. He was certain a strong spear king would challenge them, and that Opir would call out a joke or mime the king in an insulting way, or that Gorm would hurl a spear into the air and kill the king's son or brother, and all the men of *Raven* would be slaughtered. Lidsmod hoped the sailing would continue for a while. He did not want to walk on unknown land just yet—foreign, dangerous soil.

The land seemed to back up, recede, and melt away. Even with the sail up and full of the steady wind, the ship made hard progress.

It always took a long time to reach just-sighted land, Lidsmod had heard. Perhaps it was a trick of the eye, or of the mind. But it seemed this coast was actually departing from them.

Gunnar stepped back to the helm, where Njord and Lidsmod manned the steering oar. Gunnar had explained all winter that he had passing familiarity with this foreign coast from sealing expeditions; he knew it, but not well. "We're more south than we wanted to be," Gunnar said.

"I remember this river," said Njord, "from summer voyages in my youth. We never went ashore, or bothered sailing up such water." No seafaring man took serious interest in river currents—dull, earth-colored waters.

Gunnar had hoped to strike the shore a day's sail north of here and work his way along it. That's how men navigated, by roughly guessing at their destination and hitting deliberately wide of it so they could follow the current and the winds down. But it didn't matter, Lidsmod believed. A river meant towns, and towns meant treasure.

The men did an inventory of weapons. Only now were shields unstowed and displayed along the side of the ship. Some men preferred an ax to a spear. But of all the weapons, the swords were most prized. Each had a special history. Each sword was an heirloom and had a name and a legend.

There were many famous swords on *Raven*. Torsten the berserker slipped *Gramr*—Fierce—from its sheath, and let it take the sun for a moment. Ulf held *Langhvass*—Long and Sharp—into the wind, admiring the steel that had belonged to generations of his father's fathers, ever since a dwarf had forged it, shortly after history began. In a dream once, this sword had killed a giant. Ulf had told the dream to Eirik, who had made a famous song about it. Gunnar's sword, *Havati*—Keen— was famous for having cut off a Dane's arm at the shoulder in one blow.

The most famous sword of all was probably Opir's, *Fotbitr*—Leg Biter. This sword had belonged to one of the first men in Spjothof, a distant uncle who had lived generations ago. A stranger in sky-gray clothing who had been seen walking up a glacier, like a fly crawling up and out of sight, had left it plunged into the side of an immense walrus.

Lidsmod had no weapon, and no shield.

The men worked out the oars and rowed for a while. They were glad to be able to expend their excitement. The rowing felt good. There were smiles, bright teeth, and weather-reddened cheeks. They met the river current, where the wide freshwater flattened the sea swell.

Lidsmod took his place beside Ulf and gripped the oar.

Along the distant riverbanks birds rose and darted. There was nothing else—no watchmen, no sword-bearing hordes. The smell of the river filled the air. This was a broad, deep current. Njord and Gunnar had seen such rivers, but Lidsmod had never dreamed of such a quantity of sweet water. The land beyond was flat and green, and Lidsmod was sure he could smell the faint perfume of livestock and house smoke.

And more than once Lidsmod thought he caught sight of a guardsman, sun glinting off the point of his spear.

13

THEY PULLED *RAVEN* ASHORE onto a flat beach. It had not been easy to find a place where the bank was low, so it was late in the day when *Raven* left the water, shoved along by the men. Again there was a keel scar, only this time it was on foreign land.

Lidsmod knelt and pressed his hand into the river sand. It was a rich dirt, dark and silty. It held his hand-print well. The feel of it was strange. The land was flat and full of water here, Lidsmod thought. He sniffed the wind. The land was full of grass and years of fallen leaves.

Crane cut through the water and joined *Raven*. *Landwaster* approached just as darkness arrived, the dark ship coalescing out of the twilight. Men stamped their feet and congratulated each other, the three crews mixing happily.

Gunnar was impatient, but he knew that his eagerness would have to be controlled. He spoke with Egil and Berg, the lead men of the other two ships, and then gathered his own crew around him. "We need a few men to search."

That meant finding horses and food. What was necessary was a job of quick theft. Without horses, they would not be able to travel quickly over land.

"I'll go," said Gorm.

Men stirred. Gorm would need reliable companions to keep him out of trouble. Gunnar gazed around at the men, naming two more. Lidsmod guessed Gunnar did not want Gorm mixing with the men from the other ships. Many of them still hated Gorm for what he had done to Biter. However, Gorm knew horses and could handle them.

Ulf was steady, and so was Eirik. They would be able to watch Gorm and see that he did not do anything foolish or dangerous. Gunnar spoke again: "And Lidsmod."

The young man's heart leaped. Ever since he had spied the distant *Landwaster* he had sensed a growing confidence in him among his shipmates. They had always liked him, but now he had demonstrated his eyesight—and his luck. Sometimes even stalwart men had eyesight that was less than excellent. Opir the Boaster himself had once mistaken a floating, bloated sheep for a sea chest and rowed hard in his skiff through a hard rain to haul it in. Men laughed about this around the mead table, and Opir joined in with as much humor as he could muster.

Lidsmod was thrilled—and uneasy.

Gunnar took him aside and gave him a light ax, fit for cutting kindling—and for close combat. "Report to me on what Gorm does," he said quietly. "But keep out of his way."

"The moon isn't going to be up for a while yet," grumbled Gorm. "We'll fall into every puddle in this ridiculous country."

Lidsmod kept quiet and followed the three men. He thought he could smell horses, but he wasn't sure. After the sea journey this fertile land was a wealth of smells. If only it weren't all so flat. There were no features—merely wet, and trees so thick together they could not be penetrated. He smelled earth and stone. He smelled his companions, all sea and sweat.

They strode through darkness, brambles and branches lashing their legs. Gorm muttered to himself, but Gorm was masterful at keeping quiet when the time came. Gunnar had blundered, Gorm knew. He had no idea where they were. Gorm was unlucky enough to be on a gold journey that was failing before it was even started.

Searching for horses was the first thing fighting men always did. But this splashing and staggering around was like something little boys would do. A river took men deep into a country, Gorm thought. Far into it. They would not have to probe the coast. They could strike all the way into this new land. So why find horses? Gunnar did not have the imagination it required to gut this new countryside. Gorm would get what he wanted, with or without Gunnar.

Ulf lifted his hand. "We're nearly there," he said.

Lidsmod could scent it too—the fertile odor of livestock.

Gorm tested his sword, loosening it in its scabbard. He tightened his sword belt. "We won't need to use our blades," breathed Ulf, "to capture horses."

The moon was well up. Ulf gestured for his companions to wait. Lidsmod kept his hand on the head of his short ax, snug in his belt.

"What do you see?" Ulf asked Lidsmod.

In the dark was a farm. There were human dwellings; Lidsmod could not tell how many. A few. There would be dogs. Lidsmod imagined men and women just beginning to sleep. This was a dark, flat, mean place.

What a miserable little house, thought Lidsmod. Could people live in such a hovel? Most Spjothof folk would not let pigs live in such a dwelling. It was made of mud, and it was peaked like a squashed cap, so water would run down the moldy thatch. A shutter was fastened, but it hung crookedly. A line of firelight flickered.

If there were golden riches in this new land, it would not be here.

The men crept forward. Judging from the sound of sleepy conversation, humans lived in one half of the building—if you could call it a building—and the animals were kept in the other. The door half gave under a push, and the heat of animals breathed out at them. Ulf cut the thong that served as a latch.

A cow bulked against Lidsmod. She was warm and huge. Her wet nose brushed against his hand as he found a rope made of grasses and fastened it around her. Her hooves made a rustle in the straw as Lidsmod tugged.

She would not move. It was like pulling an oak. A man's voice said something, and a human figure marred the darkness. In their eagerness, the searchers had made the mistake of believing that a wall separated the human from the animal living quarters, but there was no such wall.

The mud-house dweller stayed where he was, listening. The cow began to follow Lidsmod, and it was as though a portion of the dwelling detached itself and followed him through the night. Ulf and Eirik hurried after the cow. The voice called after them, unfamiliar words, and a bloused figure ran and stopped in the moonlight. Lidsmod understood the man's confusion, and was thankful for it. What farmer expects to be awakened by four armed cow thieves?

"So," said Eirik dryly, "we can ride a cow through the countryside. We will terrify the bravest of men."

Ulf asked, "Where's Gorm?"

"Leave Gorm to his adventures," said Eirik. "A cow wasn't good enough for him. He wants blood."

The cow balked again, and Eirik and Lidsmod got behind her to push. She did not move.

"Stick her with something," said Ulf.

Eirik drew his sword and pinked her. The cow stumbled, and the rope was whipped from Lidsmod's hand as she bolted ahead of them. The men ran, Eirik working his sword back into its scabbard. A cow can be light on her feet when she feels danger, and a cow can run for a good distance when she has to. As he hurried forward, Lidsmod had time to consider the nature of cows.

He had always had a good understanding of animals, and he did not blame her for running. Still, he did not like this race through puddles splashed with starlight, and when the cow began to slow to a trot, Lidsmod was glad. This would make a wonderful poem, he considered. No doubt Eirik would add this to his *Raven* saga. The star-cow, bolting through brambles, followed by the stalwart heroes through the night.

Lidsmod snatched the grass rope. The cow rolled the whites of her eyes, and he patted her, speaking to her in the tone that had always calmed animals at home.

Gunnar ran his hands over the cow. The searchers had done the right thing, but without fire they could not roast the cow, and no man was certain a fire would be safe.

"It's a mean, low place," said Lidsmod. "No dogs, no

horses that I could see. Hardly a place fit for men." He did not have to say that there was certainly no gold.

No search was a total failure, Gunnar explained. If a man found very little, he did not have to linger where he was. Gunnar was satisfied, and said so. They would leave at dawn and travel upriver.

The missing Gorm, however, was a problem. A man like Gorm could cause alarm to be spread over the countryside. They were a small group of fighting men and would need surprise on their side.

In the first light, Njord inspected *Raven*, showing Lidsmod that the caulking between the strakes remained in good condition. Near the prow a little work with a maul and some tar was required, but the ship was sound.

The new country was a lurid green. It had been a long time since any seaman had seen such a flat, empty place. The river had been in flood recently—there were many dead trees along the bank. Terns worked the river, the white-and-black birds laughing to each other.

Opir milked the cow, and many of the men had a taste of the warm, thick beverage. Gunnar unknotted the rope and slapped the animal to encourage her to leave. "We give the cow back to the land," said Gunnar.

Lidsmod knew why. A gift looks for return. Perhaps the gods would remember this. The cow bounded out of the camp. It was not a camp now, really. Blankets were packed into sea chests. Men stood ready.

"Gorm is off riding the Westland maidens," Opir quipped, trying to sound unconcerned, "treating them like steeds."

Lidsmod could sense the tension in the men. No one wanted to be trapped here on a river shore to be slaughtered by farmers.

When a lone figure slipped from a thicket, Gunnar half drew his sword.

14

I T WAS IMPOSSIBLE, at first, to recognize Gorm.

He was muddy, all the way up his woolen leggings, and his tunic was clotted with gore. The blood was black, and even Lidsmod knew enough to reckon the number of hours since Gorm had killed.

Gorm washed his clothes in the river, careful, like all the men of Spjothof, to stay as clean as possible, rinsing his pale yellow hair in the water.

Gunnar knelt as Gorm washed, and Lidsmod could hear Gunnar's taut voice. "Every man in the land will have a sword waiting for us now."

Gorm did not answer at once. He lifted his dripping head. Water trickled down his face. "They were in my way. I was searching." Gorm knew he had more knowledge of this land than any other man now. "It was only a man and a woman, and a child. An infant. Hardly a killing. No one saw me. They'll think trolls did it."

Gorm was pleased. It had been the best night in years, he told himself. There had been sweet darkness and the smell of just-spilled blood, a smell like the sea, but deeper, richer. His sword had sung against bone. It was a delicious feeling. No man from Spjothof could be as silent as Gorm, or kill so well.

"But no gold," added Gorm. "Nothing like it. Not even copper or brass. Wood and leather, and cracked, worn-out examples of that. I spied into other dwelling huts. No horses. A few swords of no great value. I was quiet, Gunnar. They did not wake, or even stir. You wanted a search—I searched."

Every man was listening now. Gunnar asked, "No gold fortress?"

Gorm grinned at all the attentive eyes, pleased to be admired. "A fortress, and a few men asleep. If there was gold there, I didn't see it. There were goblets and other strange objects of half lead. Some were inset with stones. I cut them out. Look, here they are. This opal stone may have some value." Men had first claim to what they found, but secret hoarding was condemned.

Gunnar fingered the opal stone. It was pretty, but any Rhineland trader had offered thousands prettier than this.

"We'll be low in the water with gold in a few days," said Gorm. "I think it's a good thing there was no treasure here. This means there's even more gold in another place. They must store it all together. In a few nights, we'll be wealthy men."

The wind carried the ships up the broad river. The current was sky gray. The banks were a distant blanket of land on either side of the river. The men of *Landwaster* manned oars to try to keep pace with the other two vessels.

"They died like lambs," Gorm said. "Like rags I wiped my sword on."

The men of *Raven* honed swords, worked leather, and listened.

"They didn't fight," continued Gorm, "and the woman didn't even struggle. I mounted her, and then I cut her throat. It wasn't even pleasure. It was too easy. This is going to be so simple—we will all grow fat. We will wear out our man parts and get so lazy we won't know how to man an oar. The ships will sink under the gold—"

"Look, I'm Gorm," said Opir, "rutting everything that moves." Opir made an excellent imitation of Gorm. His eyes flicked back and forth, and his tongue hung out.

There was laughter.

"There's no need to be afraid of these people," said Gorm, steel in his voice. "They don't even have sweat baths—"

"I know what Gorm's telling us," said Opir. "He's warning us that these women stink."

Some men laughed; all were amazed. Could it be these Westland men and women never bathed? Men discussed it. Perhaps the people the four had encountered the night before had been people of little *virthing*— worth. Perhaps they had been thralls, the lowest sort of slave.

Lidsmod kept quiet, listening. He eyed the banks of the river. The entire country could not be made up of thralls. There had to be jarls and fighting men. There had to be *karls*—men who owned land and weapons and would not welcome thieves.

The wind grew weak. Every ship showed oars, the wooden paddles churning the current.

Opir gave a loud hiss. He pointed.

A river craft, with one man.

An ugly boat, a vessel like a cooking pot. The river man gawked at them briefly and then turned his attention to his own business. A roll of gray netting lay at his feet. The man plainly had seen trading ships before, and he appeared to assume that these were three sea freighters. His lack of surprise was a good sign, Lidsmod thought. Where traders came and went there was also gold coin. But then perhaps the river man was not certain about these ships—he kept looking back, his face the color of ram leather.

Njord chuckled. "We don't look quite friendly, do we?"

The river man began to row hard. It was truly a ridiculous boat, like a nutshell. *Raven* and *Crane* raced toward it, the two ships skimming the water. Trygg fixed an arrow to his bowstring, and fired the silver splinter high into the air.

It splashed beside the homely boat. The man had a peaked cap, the shape of an elbow. A man in *Crane* was spending arrows into the river too. It was a waste of arrow wood. *Raven* reached the man first, and Floki leaned between the shields and speared the man so hard that the point of the spear passed through him. It punctured the bottom of the boat, and the nutshell filled with blood and water, and sank.

No one spoke. No one was interested. The river man

was unimportant to the seamen. He had been there; they had killed him. A river fisher was dead. No one cared except, perhaps, Trygg, who cursed his bow.

But Lidsmod could think of nothing else, his grip hard on the oar. Lidsmod had never seen a man killed before.

Lidsmod saw the boatman's face, even now. His slack, suddenly death-stupid face. And Lidsmod wondered at the carefree faces of his shipmates. Did none of these suddenly unfamiliar men feel the same, sickening chill? Lidsmod felt himself shrink. His grip on the oar was weak. Lidsmod Little-ax. Lidsmod who did not want to kill.

The rowing quickened without any command.

There was a town, a squat, low town with a few low, ugly river craft. There was a tower, and a line of ugly roofs obscured by the smoke of cooking fires. It was distant, across the wide river, and no face showed to observe the three ships.

They rowed hard.

When the drab town was behind them, men muttered—too many people. But certainly a gold fortress was there. Perhaps on the way back they would share some blows with the city people after they knew how well these men could fight. They would see how badly these river women smelled.

But not now.

The riverbanks were lined with trees, and within these just-leafing trees there were almost certainly unfriendly eyes. The birdsong was sour, the pasture walls that ran along the river made not of clean, ax-sharpened wood, like the fences of Spjothof, but mist-gray, mossy stones.

It rained, and then stopped raining. The sky cleared, and there were soft clouds, white as Njord's hair. This was a very foreign sky, thought Lidsmod. This was a river-country sky. Unless they took keel to land again soon, and took some gold into their hands, the men would become uneasy.

They were parting the river water well now, *Raven* coursing far ahead of the other two ships. The very ease with which Gorm had taken lives last night made this land all the more mysterious. Some of the men began to sense a trap, and Lidsmod guessed what each oarsman was whispering to his mate: danger everywhere. They were not afraid for a moment, they convinced themselves. They were wary.

But they were growing apprehensive. The men of Spjothof did not have leaders, except for those men who were naturally most capable. If a leader became confused, or if he became tired, another replaced him. There was no shame in this. If one man could not lead, another would do the job. Gunnar, however, would be the land commander. He had proven himself against the Danes, and even Egil, leadman of *Landwaster,* listened when Gunnar spoke.

Lidsmod tried to fashion a quiet prayer. Thor was the provider of strength. He gave the fat herring, and he gave the field alive with lambs. He gave rain, and he gave vigor to the arm of man. Battle, of course, belonged to Odin, and so did the special strengths and twists of fortune that battle incurred. Poetry was Odin's, and the bear spirit of a man like Torsten. Power, sky power, and the power of the strong fist belonged to Thor. Lidsmod considered asking Eirik to fashion a song that would catch the god's ear.

Lidsmod was first to see the boy on the riverbank.

15

THE BOY CARRIED a shepherd's crook, and a dog tended the sheep.

The youth stared and ran at the sight of *Raven*. He stopped up-slope, staring hard again at the river.

The young man ran again, scattering sheep, and there was something strange about his gait, something awkward, one arm much thinner than the other. An alert shepherd, thought Lidsmod. A creature with enough wits to be worried.

Njord steered the ship toward the bank. "Smart lad," said the helmsman. "Wiser than the river man."

But the shepherd's haste had told the men of *Raven* they were close to a settlement. Even in his inexperience, Lidsmod knew that fleeing goosemaids and panicked harvesters always ran in the direction of their homes.

The afternoon sun showed fewer trees. Cattle had worn paths along the bank. The smell of hearth smoke reached the river, the odor of green, unfamiliar wood. Some of the trees had been cleared recently, the white ax cuts still unweathered on the stumps.

Raven's keel sliced river bottom, and the men worked her out of the water as far as she would go and lashed her to a big tree.

As the other ships came up, Gunnar told Ulf to search alone, quickly, and see what lay before them.

Egil and Berg did not show their excitement, but Lidsmod knew them well enough to see the blood in their cheeks.

Ulf was back before all the weapons could be unloaded from the ships. Many peaked roofs, Ulf panted, and a gold fortress. "There were men there too," he said. "Men with hammers."

"You're sure there's a gold fortress?" asked Gunnar.

"It's not finished," said Ulf, breathing more easily. "They're building a tall stone tower. Men are chiseling stone, and lifting it."

Stone walls, thought Lidsmod, testing the blade of his small ax on his thumb. There must be a great treasure to be guarded here. He looked around at the eager faces, men he had always known.

He prayed to the God of Strength that his friends might live to see night.

16

WIGLAF AND STAG had taken the sheep to the end of the abbey land. They had to pass the *aldwark,* an ancient crumbling mass of stone half tumbled into the green pasture. Aethelwulf had explained that Roman armies had built this fortress centuries ago, and Wiglaf's father had told the colorful local tale about a giant's wife needing to build a cupboard to cool her massive loaves.

Wiglaf did not peer closely into the shadows of the *aldwark.* He did not want to discover whether Roman spirits or giant phantoms inhabited the place. Forni had said he knew a pig herder who saw a skeleton warrior one Midsummer's night, grinning fleshlessly from behind a wall.

Stag did everything that had to be done without prompting. He did not have to nip the sheep. The animals sensed his presence, and the dog encircled them with an invisible cord that held them together in a bunch, the sheep seeming almost fond of their crooked-jawed guardian.

Wiglaf ate a wedge of abbey cheese at midday. As he finished, he heard the first cuckoo of spring. It was distant, far into the forest, its deliberate *you too* coming at times from more than one direction as the unseen bird turned his head one way, and then another. Cuckoos were notoriously difficult to spy.

Far away, tiny mites against the green, his father and twin brothers dragged an oak toward the village. The laboring heads of the oxen rose and fell.

Wiglaf worked the butt of his shepherd's crook into a molehill. As afternoon shadows stretched, he and the dog worked the sheep near the river, where the grass was uncropped. The sheep did not like to look up; they liked to keep their fine teeth to the field. The sheep bell clucked. The dog blinked in the sun, making his lopsided smile.

When Wiglaf saw the ships, he jumped up and ran to the bank. They were beautiful! Their sails were nearly entirely lowered, but they were white with scarlet stripes, and many bearded men rowed, the oars lashing the river white. The ships were fast, skimming the water, and shields lined the side of each boat. He could not breathe, watching such graceful speed.

Ships passed Dunwic often on their way to the city. They were always freight ships, with a few dark-tanned men aboard their slow, heavy-burdened vessels. The men on the ships rarely took an interest in Dunwic or its people. Sometimes Wiglaf would wave, and a sailor might wave back. But these three ships were not like any Wiglaf had ever seen before. These were sleek, long vessels, with more sailors than usually manned any river craft.

Wiglaf could not think of the words, but his blood and his breath answered the glory of these ships. These were like beings out of Heaven.

The men were looking at him. They had golden hair, and their eyes took him in. These were not the faces of trading men.

The rowing stopped at a command Wiglaf could just hear.

Wiglaf dropped his crook and ran. He ran across the field, leaving the sheep untended.

He ran until his side ached and his eyes wept, but he did not stop.

Brother Aelle was sharpening a quill with his blade. Wiglaf could not speak, trying to catch his breath.

"Whatever could it be?" asked the brother with a slight, lingering cough.

"Ships!" called Wiglaf. "Ships—filled with strangers!"

The brother was a scribe, an inkster of holy texts. His life was quiet, and perhaps he was pleased to be distracted for a moment by some news from the outside world. "Indeed, ships—how wonderful," he said kindly. "On the river, no doubt."

"These are not river ships!"

"How exciting!" said the brother, coughing.

"Where is Father Aethelwulf?"

Brother Aelle brushed his lower lip with the white goose feather. "He hurried forth again," he said. When he saw Wiglaf's impatience, he added, "Some further illness in the village. That mud cutter's wife you visited recently. It seems she has swallowed her tongue."

Wiglaf ran.

WIGLAF RAN HARD to his father's house and danced into the manure-scented half darkness where Sigemund was unyoking the oxen. The yoke left dark sweat patches. The ox hair was swirled and spoked, and the two beasts turned their massive heads to gaze at Wiglaf with dull curiosity.

"So, little Wiglaf comes to see his father yet again— can't stay away, can you, lad?" said his father, in a manner which was almost friendly. "And without his dog. Where's your dog?"

Wiglaf started. Stag would be hurt! But then he steadied himself. What ships would trouble sheep, or a small, lean dog? But he reminded himself that his place was not here either watching oxen give him their flat, stupid stare. He had to warn the abbot.

Being in the presence of his father always steadied Wiglaf, or at least made him cautious. Just now he began to believe that all of his worries were the concerns of a fool.

"There are ships," said Wiglaf weakly.

"Ships."

"Strange ships," Wiglaf added, knowing how pointless he sounded.

"Strange ships?" echoed his father, with something like gentleness.

"Three."

His father found the hay fork.

"And," Wiglaf continued, thinking there was no purpose in stopping now, "a ship army."

"A ship army? A ship army floated past you on the river?" His father said the words for ship army—*scip here*—with special humor. He shook hay from the wooden tines. "Is that what you saw, Wiglaf? A mighty army floating by you on the river?"

"Yes," Wiglaf croaked.

His father laughed. "Wiglaf, when I was a boy I shoveled shit. With that very shovel, worn smooth by my father's hands, God keep him." He indicated the broad, worn wooden shovel hanging on the wall. "I didn't learn how to read or how to write."

He leaned forward and spoke in a low voice. "I did things that made me strong, and made my mind clear. I didn't stand around looking at whatever happened to be floating by on the river, did I? So, what if there is for some reason a ship army? It has nothing to do with Wiglaf, or with me, or with anyone here, does it?"

But Sigemund gave a thoughtful frown as he fingered the points of his hayfork.

Aethelwulf hurried up the muddy street. "Frea is like a stone!" said Alfred the clay cutter. "Lying on the floor, her mouth agape, and going all over blue."

Aethelwulf prayed to Saint Anne, the patroness of troubled women, who understood their problems. He had to stop for a moment to catch his breath and lifted a hand to win the clay cutter's patience.

A maiden of the village was smiling from a doorway, offering him a plate of fresh-baked bread, and the abbot could not help lingering for one stolen moment, breathing the delicious yeasty fragrance. He had no time to take a taste, even though long experience told him that poor Frea was beyond all human aid.

He heard a cry and turned.

He saw the blood first. A man ran toward him down the muddy street, his face scarlet with it. The incredibly bright blood coursed and trickled even as the man ran. Blood washed the man's tunic. That a man could run with so much blood flowing from his head was grotesque. And when the man spoke, his teeth were white within the scarlet mask.

The man was an impossible apparition, jabbering at Aethelwulf. The poor creature held him with a bloody hand. It was Edgar the fowler, a man who lived at the edge of the village, near the river, where the damp earth rose up in puddles that favored the raising of ducks.

"Strangers, Father!" cried the injured man, sinking to his knees. "They're killing everything that lives!"

18

GUNNAR OFFERED INSTRUCTIONS, the men nodding as they listened.

Njord and a few men from *Crane* would stay with the ships. The rest would march with their own crews, and if there was any attack, they would form three wedges, the leadman at the point of each. Lidsmod would come with the fighting men but stay well away from the shield wall. "Protect our rear," said Gunnar. Lidsmod was being spared the greatest danger, and he was both grateful and resentful.

There should have been darkness. There should have been more information about the land that lay ahead and around them. But there was no time. They had the old advantage, a warrior's simplest trick—surprise.

Every man realized this. The bosses of the leather-covered shields gleamed in the sunlight. Men adjusted belts and worked their heads into the peaked helmets. Sword belts were loosened, and mail chinked as men settled it around their shoulders. A few men wore such mail, and some had leather guards for their shins.

Each man was ready, in his own way. Gunnar drew Keen and let her cut the air with a whisper. Ulf lifted

Long and Sharp. This ancient sword would eat its fill today, Lidsmod thought, envying his stout shipmate.

Lidsmod hefted his small ax. His limbs tingled. Every blade of grass was sharp in his eyes. The land had a smell of ripeness.

Horses were useless in battle, Lidsmod had heard. They were good only for travel over land. Two legs planted on a field were all a man needed. The shield bearers began to stride forward. No one spoke. *Raven's* men swung to the right, across a pasture. The wet earth squelched under their leather soles. Sheep stirred and began to run in that curious, easy panicked way of such animals, but the men ignored them.

Gunnar strode ahead. They would slaughter a few sheep on their way back, Lidsmod thought, for food. As much as men admired courage, no man wanted to be in a situation that required it. Lidsmod had heard the firelight fighting lore, long into the nights of his boyhood. It was always better to strike quickly, by surprise. Gunnar quickened his pace.

Gorm began to run, pushing himself ahead of the ragged line of men. Gunnar ran too, remaining just ahead of Gorm. What a sight they all were in Lidsmod's eyes. Swords, axes, spearheads gleaming, each man gaining speed.

Surely this settlement was alarmed, Lidsmod thought, surely there would be men rallying to protect it. The men from Spjothof would slaughter them all. They ran recklessly now, and this was dangerous because some, such as Ulf and Trygg, were bad runners—strong oarsmen, thick-necked and deep-chested, but heavy-footed.

A man in ugly, shaggy wool clothing stood surrounded by ducks and duck-soiled mud. The man raised a cry, and Gunnar gestured. A man from *Landwaster* cut at the man, knocking him down, then laid about him, scattering duck feathers.

A town beyond leafless trees: roofs and a half-built tower and a gold fortress, surely that's what it was. They did not even have to enter the town to find the gold! This was indeed a great gift, thought Lidsmod. And the little town itself, with its mud-yellow walls and its far-off timbered hall, did not look so poor. There would be gold in some of these dwellings. A rooster stretched his neck, his red plume arched like a scythe.

They were a surf of men, like a battle force in a saga, a sword tide.

A boy ran toward them, hurrying to reach the refuge of these stone buildings. Lidsmod recognized the shepherd with the withered arm. The youth twisted in his stride and hurried into the gold fortress.

The rooster fled, a single, copper-bright feather floating in the air. Workmen stood at the base of the stonework; one held a hammer. They wore the plain gray tunics of thralls. One or two of them might have made good slaves. These were not weak men, but they had stupid looks of amazement. One man did, in fact, wield a hammer. It was a wooden maul, though, not a mighty Thor hammer, and Gorm and Ulf made quick work of the laborers before they could rally.

Blood winged into the air, and swords made the squeal of steel cutting bone. As the stoneworkers began to fight back, hammers fumbled for and found, feet slopped in scarlet mud. One worker banged a steel rod off Ulf's sword and then ran. He easily outsprinted the heavier swordsmen, but this caused great laughter among the men from Spjothof. Battle was not a foot race!

Gunnar directed men to watch the exits of the gold fortress, lest men try to flee with gold. But above all, he directed them to watch for a counterattack. Lidsmod had heard the battle tales. Too many wise, stalwart men had died from a spear in the back. Even the men of Spjothof would kill a man from behind—it was so much easier. And so in this land of weak men, treachery was expected.

The men of Spjothof surrounded the corpses of the workingmen, stabbing the bodies experimentally, and to give steel its blood taste. Lidsmod hacked at a leg, a hairy, sweat-gleaming limb. His small ax bit the flesh and left a red slice.

Then they spread out as Gunnar directed. The door to the gold fortress was blocked, but Ulf kicked it easily aside. Would the fighting men of this country ever show their faces? Lidsmod joined a small group that entered the gold refuge.

It was nearly dark inside, with a sweet, perfumed smoke in the air. Men sometimes hid in a dark place like this, and then speared the intruders. It was a stupid way to fight, but a trapped stoat fought this way—and was often very difficult to kill, as Lidsmod knew from hunts with his boyhood friends.

Gorm wrenched open a shuttered window. Daylight fanned into the hall and ignited gold on a table at the hall's end. One of the men picked up a bench and splintered it against a wall. There were other benches, and these were splintered too.

Gunnar directed a guard to the side door. A counter-attack was always most deadly at a time like this, when men were gold-stunned. Because, without question, Odin had guided them to treasure.

GORM HEFTED a large gold object shaped like a sword hilt. It was a curious object, and Lidsmod did not like to see Gorm handling it so roughly; it could be dwarf craft and have some unknowable power. Gorm bit into it. He gave Lidsmod a smile. "Gold, pure as mare's milk," he said.

A figure had been crafted from this rare metal—a bleeding man, magically wrought. If this was a sword hilt, Lidsmod would hate to see the blade that went with this hiltlike shape, or the man who wielded it.

There were rich stones, Lidsmod knew, in the goblet Opir found, and in the mead cup Gorm held into the light from the window, laughing.

Gold everywhere! Dark pictures of men with heads of fire were, if held into the light, made of gold leaf. Floki had found an ash shaft with a shepherd's crook of gold, and there were robes that were certainly silk. This was a wealth cavern, a jewel hoard. All of this was rare and valuable, and some of it was too strange to be assayed in this hurried way.

"Bring all of it," Gunnar commanded. But it was an unnecessary directive. The men knew what to do.

Axes splintered wood. The hall was torn apart; even

the cracks between stones were scraped and tested with knives. When the hall had been searched and the contents, both useless and rich, piled outside in the late-day sun, Gunnar directed the search of the side hall to begin.

Opir held up a skin with magical runes. Gunnar ordered it taken, although he told Lidsmod it was impossible to guess what worth it might have. Ulf dragged a robed man into the dying light and cut his throat. Fireside talk in recent months had described such men, unarmed inhabitants of these treasure places. The dying man wore a wooden bleeding-man shape on a leather thong. As he died he sputtered a stream of fervent words and gripped the wooden carving hard, as though to squeeze it of its power.

Ulf hurried back into the side hall, but a scarred old seaman from *Landwaster* and another from *Crane* had just killed another three men. They had been hiding in a huge, beautifully wrought chest, crowded together, trembling, uttering pleas or curses, words unknowable but plainly magical in intent. The two swordsmen killed them quickly and without interest, then dragged the bodies outside, where they stripped them, to see how such weak men were built.

Ulf and Gorm flung open chests, emptied shelves of clay pots, and, as they stopped to thrust swords into the ashes of a central hearth, a figure rose from the dead coals. It ran as Lidsmod looked on, too surprised to seize the running legs.

Opir laughed at the sight. The small ashy figure collided with the laughing Boaster, and Opir flung it to the floor. Gunnar emptied a pitcher of water over it, and a pale boy's face squinted up at them. Then the boy was up, and his teeth sank into Opir where he had no armor, above his knee.

"It's a little weasel," Opir laughed, and he brought the butt of his sword down on the corner of the boy's skull. The youth with the withered arm went limp. "The first true fighter we've seen here," said Opir. "And I felled him. I, Opir, the all powerful."

Gorm stepped to the fallen figure and lifted his sword, but Ulf's sword, Long and Sharp, blocked the boy's body. "I want him," said Ulf.

"This? You want this boy?" Gorm was nearly speechless. A man could take a slave but, with so little space on the ships, a slave had to be chosen very carefully. Only a man of great value could be taken, and usually only if ransom were a possibility. "Look at him! He's a weak, dirty little mouse—"

"The people of this village will pay to get him back," Ulf said. "He's a magic child; why else would he be here? I'll buy him from you if you claim him."

Gunnar pushed Gorm aside. "This is a value place. Everything here, even the rune skins, must be valuable to the folk of this country. They'll pay to get him back. Keep him," he directed Ulf. "He belongs to all of us."

Gorm bit his lips and slashed a clay vessel to powder with his sword.

Lidsmod did not allow himself to show his relief, lest Gorm see. Lidsmod doubted that the boy was worth much gold. He might be magical, but who could tell in such a strange land?

"We have ourselves a mighty warrior," said Opir. "The mightiest in this mighty land!" Twin bleeding crescents marked Opir's legs.

Ulf dragged the boy outside. "Tie him up," said Opir to Lidsmod.

"Gorm will kill him," said Lidsmod, meaning: my ax and my arm will not be strong enough to protect him.

"Never!" Opir laughed. "Here is a new Leg Biter," he said, to complement the famous sword of the same name. "I'll stay with *Fotbitr,*" he said, and Ulf laughed too. They had a living Biter, like the dead horse, and like the sword.

Let Gorm touch Leg Biter, Lidsmod thought, tying a walrus-leather rope around the boy's legs. If the boy is so much as bruised, Gorm will suffer.

"Go feed your hungry ax," said Opir with a laugh, meaning: good luck with your first kill.

Lidsmod hurried to find the source of the rough cheers and taunts.

A knot of villagers had gathered on the muddy road. A stone rang off the boss of Torsten's shield. Torsten lifted his spear. He scowled and seemed to sniff the air.

Some of the dark-haired villagers continued to heave stones, and one man swung a sling. The men of Spjothof appreciated the power of a thrown rock. It was not a warrior tool, but enough rocks could batter an army. The villagers backed off, however, as soon as the Spjotmen fell into formation.

Torsten stepped alone up the road. The men of Spjothof were silent. It was a great mistake for the men of this village to make Torsten angry. A rock bounded beside Torsten, and another.

The men of the village spread across the road, making themselves more visible, the way a cat arches its back to seem big. It was a poor battle formation. The men of

Spjothof could fan out, enclose the village, and attack this inexperienced group from the flanks. Nonetheless Lidsmod had to admire their startled courage. The villagers brandished axes, and the younger ones continued to hurl rocks.

"They're delaying us," said Gunnar. "While the women and children escape, and the animals, and while they take their hidden silver or bury it in the earth." His voice grew louder. "They are stealing our gold!" he cried.

"Gold!" cried the men of Spjothof.

Ahead of them Torsten threw his spear high into the air. It glinted in the light of the late day and when it fell, it struck earth far behind the backs of the axmen in the road.

One of the villagers laughed. "Your best spearman cannot throw any better than a child," the laugh seemed to say. The taunting villager stepped forth. He was broad-chested, with hair black as ship tar. He called to them unintelligibly, shaking a fist. "Come on and fight," the man seemed to cry.

The men of Spjothof were silent. The spear act, throwing a weapon over the heads of the enemy, had consigned these men to Odin. As every man watched, Torsten began to pant. His neck thickened, and his head shrank into his swelling shoulders.

Torsten was filling with bear spirit, and the men before him were about to die.

AETHELWULF PUT HIS ARM around the fowler with the blood-gilded face.

Alfred the mud cutter knelt beside the injured man, supporting him. Everyone seemed to move slowly. The man was lucid, as injured men sometimes are, and described the strangers as "very big, but looking much like men." The man's head wound was a gash where a sword had sliced into the flesh. Aethelwulf had seen such injuries in Frankish land disputes, when as a young monk with a surly humor he had been asked by the king's men to bind their hurts.

"How many strangers are there?" Aethelwulf asked, pulling the man toward Beornbold, Lord Redwald's hall.

"Thousands!" said the man.

"Armed with sharp-edged weapons?"

"Swords, axes, spears, shields—every weapon you can imagine!" As they reached the hall, the fowler began to stumble.

Aethelwulf ordered one of Redwald's men to send word to their lord.

"This is something I cannot do, Father." The spearman was heavy with duty. The sight of blood had made him alert, but it was a wary alertness, one of concern that he might make a mistake or, with bad luck, be bloody himself before long.

Lord Redwald was in Eoforwic, the spearman said. No one knew when he would return. He was in the city to see Lord Sigan on royal matters.

Aethelwulf wanted to throttle the man, but he pushed his way into the hall instead. Spearmen and peasants were helpless without a leader. A few spearmen lounged about the hall, looking at Aethelwulf with mild interest, but the bleeding fowler won their attention when he stammered his story.

The retainers looked at each other in disbelief. It was like trying to awaken men of oak, or worse, of stone. It was like announcing that an army of skeletons had risen from their graves.

"Surely," hissed Aethelwulf, "one of you can act!"

The men murmured. They had never known an abbot to command a hall guard before. They knew Father Aethelwulf, however, as he knew them, and a young man stood up from an ale bench. "I can ride, Father," said the young spearman, a thick-necked lad called Hoc— lurching drunk, as were all the others.

"Good!" Aethelwulf tried to sound brave and confident. "Hoc the Brave they will call you. You must ride to Eoforwic. It's the most urgent ride a man has ever taken. Take my ring as passage proof. Tell Redwald we are attacked by strangers, and that men are dying like beasts."

A few of the spear guard trudged behind Aethelwulf, moving sluggishly in their still-unstrapped armor. The fighting men were reeling with ale, one of them falling down

110

as he tried to force his head into his helmet. Why, Aethelwulf thought, is everyone so slow? Even me! His own legs were trembling, and he prayed that his body would have enough strength in it for the burden of this day.

It had not taken long for the cattle to be driven, lowing, into the woods by the women and children, and for Sigemund and his sons and other field men to gather in the street mud. A bad sight lay ahead as Aethelwulf and the hall guard panted up to meet them. Smoke climbed the sky: The sanctuary was burning. The abbey would soon follow. All the brothers must be dead—and Wiglaf! Wiglaf, jewel of his heart.

The field men stirred, leaderless and angry. "We'll stop them, Father," said Sigemund. "Come on, men. We'll slaughter them like sows!"

"Wait!" Aethelwulf embraced him. What could he tell these men? To kill was a sin, and yet surely God did not expect them to stand slack-armed as their village was destroyed. "Stay here and block the road. The abbey is already lost."

"Don't worry, Father," said Sigemund. "We'll butcher them all, every one of them, and spread their guts for the rooks!"

"We want to slow these strangers down, if we can't drive them away entirely," the abbot replied. Aethelwulf looked at the uncertain, angry faces around him. The peasants were ready to fight; the spearmen were ready to bolt.

"Christ was a warrior," said Aethelwulf. "He stretched upon the tree and suffered the blows of swordsmen so that we would not be afraid. Christ did not flinch under the Romans' lash. He did not hang his head. God in our fists! Jesu in our blades! Stand across the road, good Sigemund. You are the chief here."

The hall guard looked down, unhappy to be led by a peasant.

The men of Dunwic spread across the road. There were so many strangers! But as the abbot counted them, he realized there were fewer than one hundred. Many fewer, perhaps seventy or eighty men. Bearded, yellow-haired, with flowing mustaches and gray or blue eyes under peaked helmets. Aethelwulf directed the spearmen to take positions along Sigemund, the abbot speaking as though he had been a shield carrier his entire life.

Forni, one of Wiglaf's brothers, looked at Aethelwulf and gave him a tight, scared-man's grin. "Don't worry, Father. Look—Laughs Back is eager for a fight!" Forni held forth his ax as though it were the answer to every fear. Forni began talking to his weapon, muttering quietly. Men often spoke to their axes, and plowmen named their favorite tools.

Sigemund brandished a scraping ax, a lighter weapon. Let his sons handle the tree ax and the mattock. Sigemund was heavier than they were, but would probably tire more quickly.

This shock, this sudden attack, no longer surprised Aethelwulf. Life was made of bone and blood. He was not afraid.

"Their guts to the sky!" cried Sigemund, and the men behind him cheered.

21

EDWIN THREW A STONE, and then stooped and threw another. The stones bounded among the strangers. One field lad had a sling, and the round stones darted toward the strangers like frightened swallows. What harm could they do, Aethelwulf wondered, these little orbs of rock? Edwin found a good black stone and threw it with all the power in his arm.

It struck a shield. The men of Dunwic gathered together. They were one army now. Forni lifted Laughs Back so the strangers could see it. These strangers were huge men, stout and thick-legged. They deployed in wedges of fighters, armed with axes and swords. One man detached himself, perhaps their leader, Aethelwulf thought, armed with a spear.

Sigemund, in a display that made Aethelwulf's mouth go dry, taunted the strangers. The stranger leader threw his spear high, and when it landed far behind Aethelwulf, with a strangely harmless-sounding clatter, like a mattock tossed to earth, Sigemund called, "A little boy can throw better than that!"

The men of Dunwic lifted a cheer, a taunting cry. The strangers were weak as infants! The strangers were little

113

children sucking at their mothers' teats. Were there no men among these strangers?

"Their guts for the rooks!" piped Edwin.

The leader of the strangers strode toward them alone. The rest of the strangers whooped, a sound that made Aethelwulf's bones turn to water.

The leader made his slow way toward the men of Dunwic. He was a stocky, bearded man with a shield and a sword. His beard was the color of autumn, and beneath the body leather he was wearing a shaggy black fur that hung unevenly below his waist.

The leader was taking great breaths. His chest swelled in and out within the armor, and his face was flushed. The man spread his legs and stooped forward as Edwin threw a rock, and two spears glanced from his shield. The man seemed to shrink, bunching inward, gathering.

He roared. He flung back his shoulders, flung back his arms. His teeth were white, his armored chest exposed. The man attacked, shoulders forward, shield up. He crashed into the men of Dunwic. Bodies sprawled. Spears and swords clattered on the leather shield, and the madman's sword rang against the villagers' weapons.

Spearmen were hacked as they lay tangled. Three of them died in three flashes of the sword, and as Sigemund struck the stranger's shield with his ax, he fell too. He tried to call out, but his throat let out only a whisper, a gout of air.

Edwin fell face forward into mud like a man letting himself drop into a straw bed. A spear was slashed into two pieces as it was stabbed toward the madman's legs,

114

and another spearman coughed, his death yell turning into a spray of blood. Every remaining hall guard was butchered as he offered spear or sword, stiffly, in movements filled with uncertainty. The madman slaughtered them, roaring, black now with their blood. Boy and man ate his sword, as though they were struggling, clumsily, for the next opportunity to die.

Forni lunged forward. "Laughs Back!" he called. The noble ax buried itself in the madman's shield, and the madman turned, his savage grin all teeth.

Forni ran, leaving Laughs Back, leaving father and brother in the road. Forni wept, and Aethelwulf ran with him, shocked at what he had witnessed and at the beautiful, terrifying stream of blood pulsing down Forni's legs.

An arrow glinted through the late afternoon light, missing Aethelwulf by a handbreadth.

Too far, said a voice in Aethelwulf's soul.

The woods are too far away.

22

THE MEN OF SPJOTHOF cheered as Torsten slaughtered the villagers.

Lidsmod was glad to see the ax-wielding villagers fall. But he had heard the tales of battle and knew what was likely to happen next.

The few remaining villagers ran, one of them staggering, and Torsten ran after them, still roaring. Gunnar ordered his men forward, Trygg fitting an arrow to his bow.

As Lidsmod had feared, Gorm leaped upon the bodies in the mud and slashed with his sword. He butchered as though for an evening meal. When Gorm rose from his work, the men were in pieces scattered across the road.

Gorm was disgusted. These men had no gold. He had not expected thrall-like men to wear much in the way of treasure. But they did not even have antler-ivory pins, or bone fastenings, or any of the adornments the most common man in Spjothof would wear. Their clothes were coarsely woven, their belts cracked with use. Their weapons were adequate, but hardly trophies. The armor of the dead spearmen was serviceable, but unbeautiful.

Gorm was repulsed by contact with such poverty. He hurried after the stream of Spjotmen, eager to sack the village.

Swords chimed. Gorm raced toward a knot of new spear carriers who had just run up through the village. Torsten slashed; two men fell. A spear splintered. Gorm lanced a man's unprotected side, and when a spearman turned to battle Gorm, he feinted, paused, then stabbed the man in the throat.

When the spearmen were all dead, Gorm searched the bodies, stabbing where flesh still quivered or where breath still moaned in and out of a bloodied mouth. More poverty. More worth-poor men with no adornment of any kind.

Gorm hacked at a body and kicked it, so the air groaned out of the corpse's lungs. Gorm swore to himself that he would take this impoverished country by the neck, and strangle it.

Lidsmod led their prisoner to the ships, and Njord trussed the young shepherd like a goose, with deft, ship-wright knots. "Go back to your fighting, Lidsmod," he said. "You don't want to miss any moment of the slaughter."

Lidsmod caught something in the shipman's tone. Was it possible that Njord did not enjoy the sight of blood any more than Lidsmod?

"Go on," said Njord. "It's a brave sight, sea warriors against swineherds."

Lidsmod lifted his ax and roared with the other men as Torsten destroyed a dwelling. The berserker splattered hot barley porridge all over the interior and sliced into a roof support with his sword. The blackened wood was red where he scalloped it, and as Spjotmen looked on, the timber was carved to a spindle, then a splinter, and then to nothing.

The roof groaned. Torsten attacked the walls, and mud and straw flew. The Odin worshiper roared, and soon he had gouged his way through the wall, slashing a new door cavity. He turned to another wall and sliced another ragged light hole, and then he attacked the clay pots and the iron pots and the blankets, then did battle with yet another wall.

Even a fellow shipmate would not survive in the same building with Torsten, so the others spread through the village. Floki tracked a rooster, dived and missed, and a young fighter from *Landwaster* helped him. They both fought with the rooster, until the bird was torn and they were both freckled with gobbets of rooster and feathers.

Whenever a spot of disturbed earth was discovered, men dug like dogs. Many times in the past, Danish villagers had buried gold, hoping to return. Sometimes villagers had even hurled gold into a spring. Eirik was lowered into the well on a rope.

The well was crude. A tree trunk had been burned hollow and inserted as the lining of the well shaft. This showed some little craft, Lidsmod thought, but it was a coarse, foreign method, and not pleasing to a man from Spjothof.

When they found no gold, they burned everything. They burned every loom and crushed every loom weight. They burned every blanket and every wooden tool, and threw chickens into the burning heaps and roared as the birds ascended, birds-of-fire until they could not move, living, charred things men killed and ate half raw.

There was a fury in each man because there had been no gold, no women, and no livestock for a feast. And when men were sent to the sheep pasture, they discovered that the sheep had been driven into the forest. Some straggled behind, bawling as sheep will, but the great triumph feast had been snatched from the Spjotmen, and they were angry.

Darkness.

Gunnar and Lidsmod found Torsten tearing a hole in the ground with his sword, a hole big enough to stand in. Torsten was battling the dirt, as though wanting to do combat with Frey, the god of earth and harvest. Torsten stabbed, dug, plunged, still roaring.

Gunnar waited until Torsten leaped from the hole, and then threw him to the ground. Many others were waiting for him, at Gunnar's direction. Three men fell upon Torsten's sword arm and three on his legs. Even so, Torsten climbed to his feet, men clinging to him like ants to a tree. If Ulf had not dived at Torsten's feet, the berserker would have run into fire to singe off his captors.

Fire was golden in the night, and the heat of it made a wind that streamed through Lidsmod's hair.

When Lidsmod found a leather helmet lying in the flickering shadows, he put it on. Some spearman had worn this, some hall guard who had fled, or spilled his belly to the dirt.

Lidsmod wondered if one of his shipmates would laugh at the sight of an untested warrior wearing a spearman's helmet, but when he met Gunnar's eye the leader said, "Help us Lidsmod—if we don't search quickly, some real fighting men will find us, and you'll need that helmet."

23

UNDER THE NIGHT SKY the victors fired the roofs, destroyed every mead bench, and drank green ale from earthenware pitchers.

Lidsmod returned to the ship with a newly discovered sword and scabbard. Opir hooted at the sight of Lidsmod with a weapon hanging from his belt. He laughed at Lidsmod's stride, his walk made more difficult by the weight of the blade.

Ulf knelt and took the new thrall's head in his hands. "So, my little wolf. You don't like us yet."

"He should love us as old friends," said Opir. "The boy's an idiot, it's plain to see."

"He's afraid," offered Lidsmod, unable to suppress a degree of sympathy for Leg Biter.

Torsten was carried back through the firelight, tied to a pole. He did not look like a human being. His face was clotted with blood and char, and his leather armor was filth. He growled, and his teeth glistened, reflecting the distant flames.

Gunnar had the bear warrior placed in *Raven*. The ship now around him, his head resting on the oak planks, Torsten soon began to snore.

"He fought well," said Lidsmod.

"He killed well," corrected Gunnar gently.

Men were smoke-blackened and weary. They gathered near the ships. A few horses had been found in a distant field. Berg, Egil, and Gunnar discussed what to do next. They still had surprise on their side, if they moved quickly. Two shipmates from *Crane* got into a fight, and one was knocked senseless. Other men lay half dead from guzzling the earthy ale of this village.

Gorm leaped up and down. "We must find the women! Everyone knows the women took all the gold with them!"

"They are waiting especially for you, Gorm," said Opir. "I know they are fighting over who will be first!"

"I am tracking the women!" said Gorm.

Trygg said he would go, and a few men from *Land-waster* joined in. Gunnar waved them away wearily.

"Maybe some earth spirit will teach Gorm a lesson," said Njord. There were many spirits of tree and wood, and some did not love human beings.

Lidsmod stayed near the thrall, as though guarding the prisoner. In truth Lidsmod wanted time to hold his sword, testing the grip, stabbing at the dark.

Leg Biter was tied to the helm platform beside Njord. Njord covered the boy with a sealskin. "You'll find us good men in our way," said the white-haired seaman. "You've seen us at our bloodiest. You'll see us as we really are when we sail again. You'll learn to love Opir and Gunnar and Ulf. There's no better man than Ulf."

Ulf offered the boy some charred chicken. The boy would not eat. He stared at nothing and would not respond to their voices. There was the stink of smoke in the night air. It was not the sweet smoke of kitchen wood. It was the confused, nasty smoke of destruction.

Njord chuckled at the way Lidsmod cut at the shadows with his newfound sword. "Some hall guard dropped it in his terror," Njord suggested.

Lidsmod knew this might be true, but preferred to think that the weapon had been wielded by some brave man cut down by Torsten himself.

Eirik hummed a saga tune to himself, and Opir whispered over the day's excitement with anyone who would listen. Gunnar stalked the bank in the scant moonlight, and the sleeping men coughed and kicked as they dreamed.

Lidsmod scrambled to the bank and cut a slice of goose flesh where it roasted on a spit. He returned to *Raven* and offered the meat to the new thrall.

This time the boy took the food. He ate solemnly and without any apparent pleasure.

Lidsmod felt a little uneasy now around his shipmates: especially Torsten, black and snoring. Were these the same steady-handed neighbors who had helped his mother carry water from the stream, who had sighed at the lovely sea sagas on the frosty, endless nights?

Lidsmod chided himself, and tried to get used to the weight of a sword in his grip. Soon he would be free of the mental pictures of the dying and would lounge easily about the ship like all the other fighting men, weary as though from harvesting or butchering a pod of whales.

Ulf woke and shook himself. He stretched. He was stiff, and groaned aloud that he needed the bathhouse with its steam and hot water. He knelt beside Lidsmod. "I'm going to bathe in the river. Take care of little Leg Biter. If Gorm comes back from searching the woods in anything like a dark mood, he'll cut this prisoner's throat."

Lidsmod gave a grunt, the way fighting men did, a syllable of affirmation. He stood with the sword in his hand, hoping that on this night, at least, he would not have to use it.

24

AETHELWULF WAS SURPRISED at the power of his old bones and his aging sinews. Fear made him fleet!

But he stopped running so fast when he and Forni reached the first trees of the forest, three or four distant bow shots from the village. Forni, ahead of him, hurried back to help the abbot under the great, low branches of grandfather oaks as they stumbled their way to a hardscrabble clearing where wood gatherers had stripped the fallen branches.

Aethelwulf leaned against a tree, breathing too hard to continue. He was amazed at more than his own foot speed. He had found himself with a sword in his hand back there in the street, and he had nearly used it. The pommel of the sword had been warm from the grip of the hall guard who had held it. Aethelwulf had nearly strode forward with God's might in his arm.

But then he had realized that yet another corpse thrashing the wet earth would help no one. The abbot had been ready to die, but not to take a life. He had prayed in his heart to the Lord of the universe, tossed aside the sword, and fled.

Aethelwulf and Forni ran as buck hares do, doubling back toward home. They crept along the forest's edge. The stink of burning dwellings stung Aethelwulf, and the savage voices of the strangers were in his ears, like the croaks of carrion crows.

Forni lifted his voice in a bird's cry, sounding exactly like a male woodcock. It was some sort of hunter's signal, Aethelwulf surmised. He himself knew little of wood-lore and would be happy when he could escape this maze of shadows, the haunt of unholy spirits. Even the wisest Frankish scholars did not love to stroll near a forest when the darkness rose from the ground.

Ahead, in the dim shadows, a woman stood aside from a tree, and Aethelwulf felt like crying out to her, "Don't let them see you."

But he was silent as Forni scampered toward his mother and they embraced.

All the cold night Aethelwulf sat with the band of women, dispelling rumors. No, he did not believe these strangers ate men whole and uncooked, hair and heel. No, he did not believe they sailed with a devil at each oar.

Most of these were widows now, and Aethelwulf could not decline their questions. He kept back the sad and sickening details, saying to one woman after another, "He died with courage," or "He fell proud before Heaven." How would he ever forget the sight of the madman, butchering the villagers Aethelwulf loved?

Wiglaf sat tethered in the keel of the ship. He was shaken to his soul by what he had seen: Aelle the cheerful, quiet-voiced scribe, and the other good brothers, dead. The

126

burning of God's house and—what made it all worse—the grins and laughter of these strangers.

Wiglaf had expected them to gash him with a flaying knife or rip him open with a sword. He had prayed to Jesus for the strength to endure this agony, and then he had prayed for the souls of the good neighbors who had died.

Wiglaf prayed and waited. He was roped like a gander in market, waiting for the snap of his neck. Except that a gander did not know what would happen to him, and Wiglaf did.

The morning light was bright off the river; *scir,* Father Aethelwulf would have called it—bright and glorious. Wiglaf knew he would never see the good father again. Wiglaf would be dead, and that would free him from these brutal men.

Wiglaf began to make other plans. He did not want to die, and he did not think the river would kill him. He had seen it nearly every day of his life. Wiglaf knew as soon as the water had him, he would swim masterfully. He was hesitating, but he was only waiting for the right moment.

Wiglaf had faith. His throat tightened. He would never forget Father Aethelwulf, and thought how he would smile at such an attempt. Perhaps the father watched, even now, from Heaven. Wiglaf would make him proud! He crouched against the oak planks of the ship. Soon, he thought, I will jump. As soon as the banks are a little closer.

Wiglaf prayed, and God sent rain.

When the rain began to fall on the ship, water seemed to rise upward from the river and downward from the sky, and in from the banks of the river. Each man hunched as he rowed in this world of wet.

The young man who had given Wiglaf the slice of meat the night before pointed to himself and said his name. Wiglaf echoed it cautiously, and then he uttered his own. He heard it repeated, at once familiar and foreign on the youthful stranger's lips.

Lidsmod gave a smile and stretched a blanket over Wiglaf, a hide of short hairs that rain could not penetrate. The young stranger spoke, and Wiglaf believed he could almost understand the words. "I will remember you," said Wiglaf in return.

Lidsmod smiled and looked away.

Wiglaf kicked free of the hide and let the loose tether fall. He put his strong arm over the side of the ship. A hand—it must have been the grasp of Lidsmod—clutched at his foot, but he slipped downward.

River closed over him.

Wiglaf sank. To his horror, he kept plummeting, sinking into cold midnight, although above in the lost world it was still day. He sank until he stood on the bottom. He opened his eyes, and his eyes felt pressed back into his head by the weight of the water.

This was the moment Wiglaf had envisioned—he would start to swim now. Swim! He flailed at the water and began to scramble upward, his body spinning, rolling. Gray daylight shriveled and quaked above him.

He broke the surface. Gasping, Wiglaf squinted, struggling, fighting river current, head down, sideways, up again, his strong arm churning water while his weak arm merely thrashed.

The bank was a green line at the edge of everything. It was a distant green ridge he could never reach. The current dragged him in its muscular arms, pulling him away from the bank, and if it were possible—and suddenly anything was—the banks on both sides of the river fled him and vanished. The river tossed, fluttering in his eyes, and he saw the world fill with green night. There were no clouds, and the rain had stopped.

Wiglaf was underwater. He had to breathe, but he could not. He cried out. His voice was a large, silvery, lopsided bubble, a mockery of a scream, a wobbling ghost that rose above him, joined by another, another cry distorted into a shrugging hole in the darkness.

FATHER AETHELWULF had said that Wiglaf's weak, spindly arm had been given by Heaven to remind all who saw him that God gave power even to the weak. Wiglaf had always marveled that the thin, frail hand had wrinkles in its palm and whorls on its knuckles, exactly like the muscular, normal limb.

Now it was the frail arm that struck something solid and reached upward over the overlapped planks of the ship. He began to sink, and a strong grasp seized this thin arm.

A muscular arm hooked under Wiglaf's chin. A voice called at his ear, a foreign distortion of his name. Hands lifted him from the water. His ankle struck an oar, and he was thrown to the planks.

Lidsmod panted, dripping wet. He threw himself down and knotted the tether around Wiglaf's wrists.

Men laughed.

"Thank you," Wiglaf said, when he could speak at all.

"*Tak!*" panted Lidsmod, both amused and exasperated. "*Tak!* Ha!"

The white-haired man laughed too.

Lidsmod announced to his shipmates that the slave had said *thank you.*

The rowers thought this was very funny. Wiglaf knew he had proven himself weak as well as foolish. But no one struck him. No one threatened him. Water trickled from Wiglaf's tunic, and Lidsmod gave him a red striped blanket to wear as a shawl.

Later in the day the white-haired helmsman helped Lidsmod make a hobble that fit around Wiglaf's legs and a halter that fastened to the helm platform. His hands were free. Wiglaf knew that he could escape easily. These men no longer expected him to try.

The keel brushed reeds. Water plants snapped under the thin planks. Gunnar gave a command. Eirik and Trygg swung themselves from *Raven.*

The thrall shivered under the sealskin blanket. The rain had stopped, and afternoon sun was warm in the ship. If the thrall tried to escape one more time, Lidsmod thought regretfully, they would have to kill him. He would be too much trouble to keep, just as a ram who would not stop butting would be too much trouble on a ship.

The men set up a circular camp, sentries posted. Trygg gathered firewood. Opir and Torsten and several men from *Crane* stood guard.

Gorm and Eirik slipped across the trail, into the forest. It was late in the day, and they would hunt. Gorm was glad to see Eirik disappear into the woods. Gorm wanted to be alone. He was sick of the belch and fart of his companions.

Sometimes Gorm found himself enjoying the melody of the iron-dark birds or the bright whistle of the finch. He settled himself beside a stream. There was a clearing, and a dappling of late sun. Gorm tested his bowstring. He fingered an arrow and squinted at the arrowhead. Sometimes Gorm liked to sit still for hours.

Gorm would have sent an arrow or two into the escaping thrall. The drowning boy would have died quickly. He would have floated nicely on the river. What a waste of salt cod that cripple was! he thought. He promised himself that he would find a way to kill the boy when no one was watching. It would be, Gorm thought, a gift to his shipmates. Some might think him cruel, but Gorm knew it was hard-won wisdom.

A battle-scarred buck felt his way across the forest mulch and stared at Gorm. The buck could not read the white rune of a killer's grin, thought Gorm. A buck, even a veteran of many winters like this, could not guess what joy there was in the kill. "Sleep well," breathed Gorm.

The arrow killed the buck in an instant. It fell forward, its forelegs crumpled. The buck's rear legs clawed earth, dragging the head with its grizzled muzzle. The buck fell sideways.

A deer tick hurried along the beast's flank, like a drop of steel. Already the parasite knew the host was dead.

"Well killed," said Opir.

Gorm let the buck fall. It was a heavy load for one pair of shoulders. Gorm acknowledged the compliment with a snort. "I can loose an arrow nearly as well as you can talk."

"Then you are truly a mighty hunter, Gorm!" chimed Opir.

Eirik had also returned with a buck, young and sleek. It had been well killed, too, although a throat cut had been needed to finish it. The graceful neck slumped, black muzzle brushing grass.

Gunnar knelt over the coal cusp. He shook a pale fragment of charcoal over three brown leaves. He breathed on the charcoal and it flickered, barely pink. He breathed again, and it reddened. He breathed again and touched it with birch shavings. The first wood-scented smoke lifted into the air, a sweet smell, better than summer flowers. Soon the fire crackled, dancing in men's eyes, and the venison sizzled.

Floki lifted his spear. He took a step toward the forest and turned his head to listen. He hissed and pointed into the darkness.

Someone was coming.

Hands crept toward sword hilts. Grips tightened around spears.

Ulf appeared out of the darkness. Floki's spear fell across him, blocking his way, and its shadow broke in a folded line across his chest.

"Look at you," laughed the big bald-headed man, glancing around at the camp. "An army could cut off your heads and hand them to you."

Gunnar and the other two leadmen took Ulf aside. Their voices were low. Venison spat over the fire. Men leaned forward, eating hungrily and trying to overhear what Ulf was saying.

The leadmen were finished talking. Ulf knelt by the thrall. "How is our little Leg Biter? Still alive, I see."

He listened to the story of the thrall's escape seriously. "I wonder if you are brave, little Leg Biter, or if you are another fool."

"He's brave," said Opir. "Like Opir himself, only he can't swim any better than an ax head."

"Or any better than you." Ulf smiled.

"Wiglaf can't swim at all," said Lidsmod.

"But he knew that, surely, when he took to the river." Ulf studied the thrall. "He wants his old neighbors, not his new ones."

"He thanked me for saving his life," said Lidsmod.

"He thanked you!" Ulf leaned back, impressed. The men of Spjothof took a poor person's thanks, a dignified gift of words, seriously. "Perhaps he is not stupid. A life is worth something—a walrus ivory pin, or a whistle, at least. But this thrall has nothing to give but his good speech."

Ulf fumbled in his tunic and brought forth a bone whistle. He played it for a moment, and every man hushed at the tune. It was a song precious to Heimdall, the mysterious god who was the father of all men. It reminded them all of their home.

Ulf played for only a short while. He studied the thrall for a moment. "You see, little Leg Biter—we can do more than kill. When you learn to speak true language, you will learn things to make you proud."

Wiglaf drank in the strangeness of these men. They were like a race of golden bears, and everything they did surprised him. One man would laugh like a forest devil, and another would give Wiglaf a piece of meat—with a smile, like an old friend. Lidsmod would talk in a reasonable voice, and then Gorm would mutter what sounded like a curse, and a man with a singing voice the good abbot would have admired would break into song.

The whistle and the exotic, sour tune had surprised Wiglaf most of all. There was something startling, unpredictable in the nature of these men. Wiglaf prayed to Father Aethelwulf in Heaven for the courage to survive these brutal, confusing strangers as the whistle started up again, and the man with the glorious voice sang.

"Sleep well," said Gunnar to all of the men. "Ulf reports there is another village half a morning away."

"It has a gold fortress," said Ulf, pausing in midtune. "A much bigger fortress than the last one. There were no men in the fields. No women in the streets."

"They'll sleep badly tonight, shivering in the spear hall," said Opir.

The men agreed. The village would not sleep tonight, but the men of Spjothof would.

"More fighting tomorrow," said Lidsmod to the thrall. He doubted Wiglaf could understand, but it eased Lidsmod's anxiety to tell him. "More fighting, and more blood. I think I am becoming used to it."

"Tomorrow," said Gorm, "we will make a blood eagle!"

"Yes!" said Torsten. His voice silenced everyone. He had not spoken since he had been filled with bear spirit. It was as though an oak had spoken. "Blood eagle!" rasped Torsten.

Gunnar poked the fire. "Odin, be our guide," he muttered. Lidsmod had heard the old lore of the blood eagle. Gunnar and other leadmen had spoken of it at the ale table, describing it as an ancient practice, rarely actually employed.

"We will take the jarl," said Gorm, shaking his fists, "and make an eagle of him for the glory of Odin!"

26

THE STARS TREMBLED in the sky, as though suspended in water. The river whispered. Lidsmod found a seat beside Njord in the darkness.

"Men like Gorm have their part to play. Don't worry yourself," said Njord to Lidsmod. "Some men think that someone has to suffer or the gods are not happy. To live is to pay. Some people say so, and it may well be true."

Lidsmod did not tell Njord that he thought Gorm's love of violence had little to do with any divinity. Njord's weathered, sunny outlook would never understand a man like Gorm, who was valued for his courage, if little else. Gorm had always been a quiet, aloof man, but the folk of the village remembered how Gorm beat a rival with his fists when a beautiful woman, gifted at weaving, declined his attentions. Gorm pummeled youths who beat him in footraces, and was so quick to ask payment for gambling debts that some men refused to sit at the feasting table with him.

And yet Gorm had a touch with horses; despite his roughness, animals trusted him. This meant a good deal to his neighbors, who believed that animals, like spirits, could judge a man's virtue. Lidsmod hoped that the coming battle would place him close to Gorm, where the bitter man's uncanny sword work would protect his shipmates.

A man shape climbed into the ship. Ulf said nothing, fumbling for his sea chest. Starlight gleamed off his bald pate as he hefted a honing stone in his palm.

"Keeping Long and Sharp nameworthy?" asked Njord.

Ulf gave the customary affirmative grunt of Spjothof. The dark shape of the sword left Ulf's scabbard. The honing stone rang on steel.

"Tighten the knots on the thrall," said Njord to Lidsmod. "Gorm might convince the men they need to practice the ancient art. Who will make a better blood eagle, Gorm will ask, than the new thrall?"

The Spjotmen were in the ships long before dawn. The black shapes of the prows cut through the last stars. The men rowed silently.

Lidsmod was happy to row. He was convinced he was ready to kill, and he believed that today there would be more of a battle than in the first village. Torsten would not be able to kill an entire town ready-armed against him. In these times anyone could find himself swept into the Slain Hall, and this thought made the rhythm of the oars in the darkness especially chilling.

Sometimes men cast lot twigs before a battle to discover whether they would live or die. Near Spjothof there was a special place, a shallow cave outside the village, where a seeker could talk to dead men. The spirits listened, and gave their answers in dreams. This was a spiritless land, however, as far as Lidsmod knew. A dream here was likely to have little meaning.

The sun was not warm. Its light was like a bitterness in Lidsmod's mouth and in his entire body, thumb and bowel.

Gunnar turned and waved to the ships behind them. *Raven* sliced a wake to the riverbank, and the men dragged *Raven* up a beach of silt. The other ships joined the newest of them. Soon armed men tested their shield grips and stamped against the cold.

Gunnar spoke, and the men were silent. The men of *Raven* would slip though the forest, where Ulf had spied the village the day before. The rest would march directly up the road along the river. The plan of attack was an ancient one, the Crab, in which a large pincer and a smaller one closed on a foe.

Men adjusted leather straps. Some had been decorated with scarlet paint, because of all the colors, the finest in the world was red. Men straightened their helmet linings, the wool inner cap under the leather. Thongs were untangled, belts cinched. Before sunset the evening before one of the Spjotmen had seen a man dressed like a hunter, with a bow and quiver, running along the river as fast as he could, away from the Viking ships. Certainly the fighting men of the next village had spent the night in preparation.

Lidsmod, wearing a helmet and carrying a sword but no shield, felt icy. He did not speak or meet any man's eyes. His sword caught sunlight prettily enough, but the hilt was wrapped with sheep's hide, many times around, as though its most recent owner had much smaller hands than an earlier, perhaps long fallen, bearer of this weapon. Like any youth of his village, Lidsmod had hacked with wooden swords and knew the basics of blade work. He also guessed that this heavy, capable weapon was destined to have no excellent repute. Nevertheless he spoke to it under his breath, as was normal for a fighting man, and asked the sword for its loyalty, thanking it for finding its way into his hand.

Njord would stay with the thrall. "If he tries to escape," Gunnar said to Njord, as he ran a finger across his throat so that the thrall would understand.

Njord flourished a fish-scaling knife. "Chin to hip, like a haddock." Njord held the knife in his teeth and tightened the boy's tether so that such gutting would not be necessary.

Two men from *Crane* would stand guard. It was dangerous to leave such a light ship guard, but every hand was needed. Even my own, thought Lidsmod.

"Lidsmod, you'll win a shield today." Ulf grinned.

Gunnar lifted his sword, and the men of *Raven* followed him into the forest.

27

AN EMPTY FIELD STRETCHED between the forest and the village. The earth was dark, recently plowed, clods gleaming.

The village was deserted, but the spear hall just beyond the town was closed tight, all of its shutters sealed; a breath of smoke lofted from the center of its roof.

Ulf slipped and fell into the mud, but the bulky warrior was soon on his feet again. Men grunted with the weight of leather armor and with the weight of their own muscle as they quickened their pace, approaching at a trot and, at last, an all-out run.

No fighter met them. They swept through the first dwellings. Doors and shutters splintered. Pots were dented or crushed. It did not take long to determine that these houses were empty and that they held no treasure. Someone started a fire in a thatched roof, and it smoldered, the wet stuff burning poorly.

A dog yammered at them, and Floki lanced it. One moment it was barking, and then it was not. It had been a yellow dog; now it was red. The spear pinned it to the mud.

The dog was the only warrior visible. Pig wallows were abandoned; goose pens held only feathers. The men from the other two ships swirled about, and Gunnar called, "The gold fortress!"

This gold fortress was near the center of the village, as though to seek protection from the houses around it. It was larger than the first gold fortress, and also better timbered. It had a stone tower, but this tower was complete, as thick around as four hall oaks, and nearly as tall. Opir and Trygg axed the door to white splinters, and even then they had to chop at cross timbers that blocked the way.

Steps echoed.

The hall had been stripped. Nothing gleamed; nothing caught the unshuttered sun.

Gorm danced up and down. "They have stolen it! They have stolen all of it and dragged it to the great hall where they are all hiding!"

This was, Lidsmod guessed, probably the truth. A cry rose. "To the hall!" the men called. Warriors streamed toward the hall, a tide of armed men.

An earthwork barrier surrounded the building, a low, sloping wall, the height of a man. It was not tall enough or in any way imposing enough to be impressive. Even as the men charged up the modest slope to the seemingly empty moat that surrounded the hall, the earthwork did not look dangerous.

But a dozen helmets appeared at the lip of the barrier, and black arrows filled the air. A spear hummed past Lidsmod, and another punctured Eirik's shield. He was unhurt, but paused to shake the spear free of his linden-and-leather shield. Gunnar called out a command.

Ulf was the first to see what Gunnar wanted. The two ran around the hall and leaped into the moat behind the earthworks there, as Lidsmod joined them. The hall guards here were not children. They were trained men, who had been told to wait until they were attacked. A great jarl, Lidsmod reasoned, must command this hall. Only the men of a proud jarl would fight so well.

Ulf and Gunnar both staggered under the blows of sword and spear, and Lidsmod fell backward. He was on his feet at once, but could not find space to swing his blade. It was the first fighting Lidsmod had ever shared, and yet he did not take a moment to notice what was happening, to shape it into story verse. Other sea warriors crowded behind Lidsmod, but only three or four men could stand side by side within the earthwork.

These guards had frightened brown and green eyes, and pale, tight lips. They began to hesitate. They were afraid to strike further lest they leave themselves open for counterblows. They were disciplined, Lidsmod saw, but he doubted that they had ever killed before.

Gunnar crashed his shield, boss against boss, against the shield of the tallest man. The man pushed back, strong-legged and stubborn. Gunnar's sword sliced through the air in a circle and rang into the man's helmet. Keen had done its work. No helmet of iron and leather could stand up to a proud sword.

Still the stubborn man did not fall but fought back, sword against shield. Gunnar struck three more times before the swordsman fell, his dark skull matter bursting from his helmet.

Ulf killed a guard with one blow and then, as he struggled to free Long and Sharp from the sinews of a neck, another man stabbed at him with a long blue sword, and another, with a dark, forked beard, slashed with a shorter knife, neither man strong nor accurate, but together troublesome.

Ulf took a deep breath and gave a great cry. "Spjothof!" he cried, so that the men of this place might know the name of the village their slayers came from. At the sound of the name of Ulf's home, the blue sword came alive, and Ulf pressed his enemy to the wall.

Lidsmod stayed close to his oar mate, sword heavy in his hand. Ulf hammered with shield and blade. A shield could be an excellent weapon, and Ulf knew how to use it. He struck with his shield and struck with his sword, in an alternating, relentless rhythm.

Lidsmod struck at a shield thrust before him. More hall guards crowded around Ulf and Lidsmod, driven around the hall by the attack of the Spjotmen. Lidsmod fought blindly, Ulf beside him, both of them attacking a blur of iron and leather. Lidsmod could not draw a breath to cry the name of his home. Both men staggered, their shields hammered by ax and sword. Their backs were to the earthworks. Let Frey support them, prayed Lidsmod, the earth power at their backs and in their legs.

Blood whipped across shields. A human bear roared, and steel cracked into bone.

28

TORSTEN WAS AT WORK, slashing, ripping. Three men down, then five. Gorm appeared beside him, slipping past Ulf and Lidsmod. Gorm killed quickly, silently. He stabbed at throats, thighs, crotches, plunged at eyes, butchering men as they buckled.

There was a cry above them. A white-haired warrior stood on the roof of the hall. He lifted a sword and called to his men in their tongue, speech the Spjotmen could nearly understand. His men fought harder now, and yet Torsten slaughtered them easily. Gorm too had little trouble, parrying, lunging, dirt churned to blood-soaked mud at his feet.

The white-haired warrior called again, urging his men. Gorm laughed and leaped, grasping the edge of the roof with one hand, clutching at the thatch, hauling himself up and onto the roof.

The white-haired warrior turned to face Gorm. The old man had a sword in his hand but carried no shield. Gorm straightened in surprise. The man's eyes were white with milky film. He was blind—Gorm was about to fight a blind man! This, Gorm knew, was the great jarl who had planned this defense. This was the proud man who would be sacrificed to Odin. This would be the blood eagle.

It was too easy. Gorm stepped to the nobleman's side. The old warrior was not weak, but Gorm closed his hand over the man's sword fist and tripped him. The jarl fell, staring about with his sightless eyes.

The hall guard ran, struggling over the earthwork, fighting to escape. They ran toward the forest; many of the Spjotmen followed, although the fleeing men were fast and reached the forest long before the Spjotmen could catch up.

The silence was a shock.

Birds cheered in distant trees. A black bird, nearly like a raven, called at the far edge of the sky.

"Bind Torsten," Gunnar snapped. The berserker struggled, and more men fell upon him, holding him down. At last Opir joined in, and Torsten stopped roaring.

Lidsmod surveyed the blood-slicked dead. His sword was hacked in one place, a silver nick. A man had slashed at Lidsmod and Lidsmod had stabbed back, striking nothing. But he was satisfied. He had been attacked, and had fought back.

It was enough for an evening tale. "He attacked me, sword against sword, and I stood my ground," Lidsmod would say during a long fireside winter years from now.

But the battle had been nothing like a saga. The wounded had bawled. Men had fought bravely only until they could run. Spearmen had wept. Men had died quickly, or had been hacked bit by bit.

"Find yourself a shield," said Ulf.

146

This was not the Ulf that Lidsmod knew. He was spattered with gore, and he looked larger than the usual Ulf—swollen, powerful. It was eerie to hear the voice of Lidsmod's friend coming from this battle beast.

Lidsmod could not speak. He had seen Ulf at work, killing. He felt he did not know Ulf again, or any of his friends. And he did not recognize the great feeling in his heart—exultation, half composed of relief that he was unhurt, and half heady with pride. Their enemy had run so hard!

"Here's a stout leather-and-bronze shield," said Ulf kindly, showing Lidsmod how to wrap his fingers around the grip.

The hall door was made of black timber. Opir and Trygg axed it, the high sweet song of steel twisting in wood resonating as men watched, swords poised. There was a roar as the door fell inward, and the Spjotmen stormed the hall.

But quickly they ran out again, spears clattering behind them, a band of defenders still maintaining a stronghold deep within the interior.

Lidsmod panted beside the door. A spear had just missed him. The shaft had whispered into his ear like the lusty woman he dreamed of sometimes, whispering his name as he mounted her. He was giddy with the knowledge that he had nearly eaten a spear, and he crouched for a moment outside the hall, feeling a shaky sensation very much like joy.

"Three men could hold off a hundred," said Ulf.

Gunnar considered. He lifted Keen. "Follow me!"

Lidsmod did not look back. Perhaps two men followed Gunnar, perhaps thirty. Lidsmod lifted his all too heavy blade, and rushed the darkness.

A spear slammed into Lidsmod's shield. The point punctured all the way through the wood, and the weight of the spear dragged the shield down. A spear sang off Lidsmod's helmet, a sharp, painful blow. He struck at nothing, and at nothing again, whirling, slashing, until he met iron with his sword.

The Spjotmen were with him then, and it was quick work. There were only a handful of hall guards, boys and withered, scrawny men whose heads rattled in their helmets. They fell at once. There were five men in black robes, men from the gold fortress. They knelt, offering their heads to the steel; two men from *Landwaster* killed them.

Later Lidsmod wondered if he had touched flesh with the edge of his sword, and told himself that he had nipped a forearm and cut a helmet so badly that the man wearing it cried out.

He had not killed, but each breath was wonderful—he had survived!

Riches.

It was like dream gold, beautiful, seeming to radiate silence and power. The flames of the hall fire glittered in the gold and garnets and sapphires. The arms of the seafarers were laden with the heaviness of treasure.

"But no women," Opir taunted Gorm. "The women knew that Gorm the stallion had arrived. They ran away!"

But the gold was enough to please anyone, Lidsmod

148

thought. Men carried it to the edge of the village, where Eirik sorted it at Gunnar's direction. There were figures of the bleeding man; images of golden suns bearing faces with dark eyes; images of torture—of suffering, gashed sides. This was solemn treasure, the treasure of a people who had seen violence and understood it. But there was something more here, a presence Lidsmod could not name. If the men and women of this field-strewn land paid homage to this tortured figure with nails through his hands, perhaps these treasures had power.

Perhaps some unknown divinity guarded such hoards. These images must have some magic, Lidsmod considered uneasily. Black-robed men alone without weapons could not think to protect these golden, hilt-shaped objects. Lidsmod's mother had told him tales of mountain sprites and of the voice of Thor itself in thunder. Lidsmod guessed there was some charm at work in these golden prizes, or some spirit that defended them.

These sheepskins covered with runes, these chalices blistered with opals and amethysts—Lidsmod did not trust these objects. Perhaps the Norns had special love for such gold themselves. The figure they saw dying on the sword hilt of gold: what could he be but someone who was being tortured? Perhaps he was a warning that whoever stole this gold would suffer such a death.

"Blood eagle!" cried Gorm.

The old jarl was dragged, bound and naked. His white, wrinkled body was tied to a post. His hands were lashed before him, around the green wood pole, and Gorm approached, his sword bright in the sun, to make the eagle.

Men gathered, cheering. Odin had been generous—

149

there had been great slaughter, and not a single Spjotman hurt. The men knew that Odin would love the death of this great jarl. This man was blind, a handicap Odin would appreciate, and he had been brave. This was a worthy foe, and a fit gift for the one-eyed god.

Gorm stabbed the man along his spine and cut downward. The man bellowed in pain. Blood gushed. Ribs snapped. Gorm stabbed into the back on the other side of the spine as the old man slumped, and sawed easily through rib and muscle.

Gorm spread the wings, opening the man like a shuttered window, the ribs spread wide, the lungs dripping black.

The Spjotmen cheered.

Lidsmod raised his voice too, his ragged cry a prayer to the god that spared young warriors from the blade.

29

AETHELWULF LED THE WOMEN and children out of the forest and back to their village.

Dunwic was not a dwelling place any longer. Few walls were still standing. Smoke rose from stones. Charred sheep bones littered the road, and the mud was dark with the blood and remains of husbands and fathers, their mortal flesh, spoiled under the sky, probed by blue-black crows.

The dead were buried by Aethelwulf and the grieving women, working with the mattocks and a charred shovel. Aethelwulf prayed, and the women prayed with him. The abbot spoke of the promise of God's solace like a man walking a path he knew well, a trail he could follow blind.

Eadgifu, Wiglaf's mother, approached the abbot when he thought no one observed him blotting tears with his sleeve. "My Wiglaf was the son I gave to God," she said. "For God to save and keep in His hand's hollow."

For a moment Aethelwulf struggled to think of words of consolation, some way of giving strength to this worn, stout woman.

"I believe he is there still, good Father," she continued. "Wherever Heaven has found him."

Was it possible, thought Aethelwulf, that this peasant widow was offering him comfort? Had he returned to the pride of his youth, when he thought of women as little more than keepers of the hearth or pleasure givers? Because it was true that, so many years ago, Aethelwulf had tasted carnal joy. He was ashamed of himself for thinking so little of womenfolk even now. "Eadgifu, you are wise," he said.

"Oh, no, Father Aethelwulf, not myself," she responded, as though embarrassed by his praise.

"Wise in your love," he said. "Which I have read in books," he added with gentle irony, "is the only power that matters under Heaven."

So many people remained, and they all depended on the old priest's strength.

Even a few men trickled in from the woods—hunters who had been far beyond the river, woodsmen who now mourned their fallen brothers. The abbey walls remained standing, blackened and roofless. The fallen timbers of the roof were scaled and silvery. Aethelwulf asked God to make him strong, as wholehearted as the peasant widow. He made the blessed Sacrament from coarse barley meal, and he found an only partly shattered firkin of wine.

Later Aethelwulf searched among the ashes. Something rustled at his feet, and he stooped. It was an ampulla, a fire-stained flask. He stooped again and discovered a pyx, the box for the Sacrament. The pyx was brass, not gold, which was why it had not been stolen. It was still warm from the fire it had escaped.

He was not hunting for cast-off or neglected treasure. He was hunting for Wiglaf's bones. He grieved for every person who had died. But his own special, personal loss, was the eager young shepherd.

The abbot's faith was sturdy. But he had been shaken by what had happened in a way he had trouble putting into words. He had seen himself with a sword in his hand, ready to take a life. Certainly Jesus, who had warned against the sword, could not have loved this sight. But Aethelwulf could not have stood by and let his sheep be slaughtered. Didn't men have a duty to fight for their children?

The survivors could eat the mutton of the sheep that some were already gathering from the fields. They could slaughter an ox or two. But so much of the stored barley had been burned—all but a few measures of it. This would be seed barley, and it was past time, nearly, for the planting.

Redwald would have to buy peasants, or their labor, from another lord. There was a future, Aethelwulf consoled himself, but it would be hard.

When would Lord Redwald receive word of this, and when would he ride from the great city with an army large enough to protect them all? Because the strangers had rowed upriver, by all accounts, and they would pass this way again.

A spring rain fell. Work could cure even grief. Aethelwulf went from person to person, encouraging them, helping to set up canopies against the rain. They had few blankets, but certainly, he told everyone, the cold weather was long behind them.

Firewood had to be gathered, cows milked. Buckets

could be salvaged. Aethelwulf thought of Wiglaf and closed his eyes against tears.

When they heard the rider they gathered together, ready to run for the forest. The hoofbeats thudded from up-river, from the direction of Hunlaf's village and the king's fortress in the distant city.

It was all the worse when they did not recognize the horseman, his steed sweating, trembling with exhaustion.

"Father Aethelwulf?" said a voice from the mud-dark face, a city man's accent.

"I am he," said Aethelwulf. And he added the ancient welcome formula: "And you are welcome to our bread and to our board."

He meant no irony, but the rider gave a doubtful smile as he eased from his saddle. "I have word from Lord Redwald."

Such messages were formal and always memorized, down to the smallest detail. Aethelwulf responded with the timeworn permission to speak: "I await your tidings." He was inwardly certain that this message pertained to ordering the slaughter of some bullock or arranging a gift of candle wax to the abbey, or some equally irrelevant request sent on its way long before the village had been lost.

"Lord Redwald has heard your message of the strangers from the river, and the fires, and the blood upon his soil," said the messenger. "Lord Redwald assures you that he is riding forth with an army that, with the blessing of God the Almighty, will cast these wicked men into the river that brought them."

Some of his old youthful impatience returned to

Aethelwulf now—anger and pride. "The distance one man can ride, an army could travel in the same number of hours."

To his surprise, the mud-soiled man knelt at the abbot's feet. "Father, King Aethelred swore that such strangers attacked only for church gold," he offered in his city English. "No one believed they would harm good village folk. What I have seen, passing through Lord Hunlaf's land—" Real emotion, or a failing of his descriptive powers, choked the messenger for a moment. He continued at last, "I have never seen so much blood on the ground."

The Devil loves sarcasm, so Aethelwulf controlled his tone when he said, "I look forward to welcoming Lord Redwald's army."

30

SMOKE ROSE STRAIGHT INTO THE SKY.

Gunnar directed that all the gold be placed where Eirik and Floki worked, sorting the gold and wrapping it into blankets. There was a blanket full of golden cups and silver plates, and another glittering with candleholders. Lidsmod took pleasure at the sound the heavy treasures made, heaped together.

Men swung the slain into the fire, and the burning bodies gave off their own heavy blue smoke. This burning was not done mockingly, but as a matter of no consequence. It was proper for the dead to be burned, and useless to leave them underfoot. Lidsmod could feel the heat, even where he stood near the gold, far from the fires.

Opir flushed out a goose, a big, angry bird. Perhaps it had been in the forest, with all the other livestock, and had not, in the nature of geese, wanted to remain hiding. Opir ran after the bird, waving his sword. The bird dodged, honking, easily escaping Opir, who began honking after the goose, trying to woo it.

Lidsmod had to laugh. How gooselike Opir was! Or perhaps the goose was Opirlike.

156

Opir surrendered. He fell to the ground, his arms outstretched. The goose was too quick for him.

Two men from *Landwaster* tried to tackle the large fowl. It eluded them and left them laughing in the mud.

"Leave the bird to me," said Trygg, selecting an arrow from his quiver with care. He nocked an arrow into the bowstring. This was a special arrowhead, a scythe-shaped head, and Trygg did not hurry his shot. The bow bent. The goose ran, neck outstretched, white feathers drifting behind him.

Trygg's bow made a single, musical note. The goose ran, its neck outstretched but pink now, with blood. The bird fled headless, the white wings spread, the bird running silently as men laughed until they had tears.

Lidsmod wanted to avoid looking in the direction of the blood eagle, where the corpse stood, its black wings spread to the sky. The sight blanched Lidsmod, but he could not keep from stealing glances in its direction. He had not guessed that gods and men could be so cruel.

"No one enjoys their first battle," said Gunnar.

"This has been a good day, in every way," Lidsmod said, trying to believe it. And he did, for an instant.

"I love battle," said Gunnar frankly. "But this—" He made an exasperated gesture. "This smoke and heat—"

Like most men of Spjothof, Gunnar did not care to put deep feelings into words. But Lidsmod recognized a change in the leadman's manner toward him. Gunnar spoke now as to an equal.

"This is not like sailing under the wind," suggested Lidsmod.

Gunnar gave a soft laugh, and Lidsmod could see why

his mother enjoyed sharing a cup with this quiet man. Gunnar said, "The men will be tired soon."

The hall was burning well now. Most gathered around the burning *skali*, although a few watched bright-eyed as Eirik inserted poles into the carry loops in the chests. A few men staggered, ale-crazed, and the steersman from *Crane* urinated into the burning hall, the amber arc hissing as his companions laughed.

When a spear lanced through the windless sky, it looked like a spear thrown carelessly, in exuberance at the sight of the blaze and the tremendous booty. Another joined it, and it seemed like another spear tossed recklessly in exuberance.

A short, dark spear fell through the crook of Opir's arm as he pulled feathers from the goose, and he looked around angrily. "That nearly hit me!"

Someone, Lidsmod thought, was throwing with a very thoughtless aim.

An oarsman from *Landwaster* stumbled away from the hall fire, a long, yellow shaft protruding from his side. Surely, Lidsmod thought, this was a trick of the eyes. Surely this was not what it appeared to be.

The man fell. He opened his mouth and belched a fountain of bright heart blood.

The men from *Landwaster* gathered around their fallen sea mate. Men stirred stupidly. Ale dumbness made them slow as yet another spear hummed through the smoke.

Only then did they hear Opir's voice, high-pitched over the thunder of flames, calling for help.

158

31

OPIR FOUGHT at the edge of the village; Lidsmod and Gunnar tugged their swords from their scabbards as they joined him. Opir the Boaster was a nimble swordsman, and as he let out a high war whoop that froze his assailants, it was clear to Lidsmod that Opir fought almost as well as he could talk.

These English fighters were dark men, with dark leather and brown hair. A half dozen men, Lidsmod thought. Two or three had boar-head helmets. One wore a helmet of shiny metal, well forged, chased with iron. They pounded Opir to the ground, hammering the boaster's shield with their sword edges, the sound loud and sickening.

More dark-mailed men arrived, faces flushed, eyes glittering. At last Gunnar's men formed a shield wall. Gunnar fought hard, shield and sword, the shield wall forcing forward, driving the attackers away from the recumbent body of Opir. Lidsmod knelt over the still-breathing Opir as Gorm joined the front line, blood winging into the sunlight.

Lidsmod shook his fallen friend.

Opir blinked. "I lie down when I am tired," he said weakly.

Lidsmod's sword arm was burning, already weary, but he knew that his inexperience kept him from doing any harm to the enemy. He fought with his entire body, from his toes to his helm, throwing his entire weight into each shield clash, but he was not heavy enough, or canny enough, to do more than keep his place in the front.

Men from *Landwaster* and *Crane* filled the half-drunk, exhausted battle line. The fire of the village burned behind them, and Lidsmod could see for the first time that these attackers were far less weary than the seamen. Several were clean-shaven, but the jarl was a man with a bright red beard, calling out orders in the half-familiar mishmash of sounds that passed for speech in this land. Ulf threw two of them to the ground, and while they struggled to rise he killed them, driving the point of his sword into one throat, then the other.

A spear shattered, and a splinter as long as an arm lanced Gorm's thigh. It was not a serious wound, and Gorm laughed. He laughed again, and fought harder. But there had been a moment when his sword had hesitated, and Gorm faltered, shaken.

Lidsmod was aware that this was a battle right out of a poem. He did not allow himself to acknowledge the fear that weakened his legs—something close to panic—or the strange ecstasy too, the satisfaction that came from driving a shield backward, fear in his opponent's eyes. Eirik was bleeding, an arrow in one arm. He began to sing the saga of the one-armed warrior who battled an army of giants. Gunnar closed in beside Eirik and told him to save himself.

But the poet lifted his voice in another song, a sound that must have chilled these boar-headed attackers. The song was an ancient one, handed down by generations of Eirik's forefathers; it told of the heartwood of Spjothof, how no ax could slice it through.

One seaman was down, and then another. Sea mates dragged them to their feet, but the Spjotmen crumbled. Careful to help the wounded and retrieve fallen swords, they did not panic, but they did not stand and fight. They turned to taunting. They bluffed and beckoned, inviting these landsmen onto the points of their swords.

But these landsmen were disciplined, and followed their jarl's directions. They did not hurry. They kept together and closed deliberately around a small knot of men, including Gunnar and Lidsmod.

Ulf and the bleeding Eirik stayed at Gunnar's side. They called to other men, and together they formed a *skjaldborg*—a shield fort—around their chief.

Swords slammed shields. The shield fort buckled, then pushed back. Poems told that it was as hard to penetrate a shield fort as it was for a hound to break a hedgehog's neck.

Gunnar called out, "To the ships!"

Lidsmod too raised his voice: "To *Raven*!" As though the sound of the ship's name was enough to save their lives.

32

WIGLAF HID INSIDE THE SHIP, but even there he could see the smoke rolling into the sky. He could clearly hear the cries of the strangers as they celebrated the terrible thing they had done. Wiglaf had caught only a glimpse, climbing high onto a sea chest, but he could not drive the image from his mind. The tortured figure of Lord Hunlaf was obscured now by burning thatch.

How long, Wiglaf wondered, before they do such a thing to me?

The old man who stayed in the ship was named Njord, another odd name. The sound of the name was soft and curled, like a lock of white hair. Wiglaf liked saying it, and he convinced himself that Njord was not as dangerous as the others. Njord was working with a knife, carving on a large white tooth. Wiglaf had never seen a tooth this big. It was nearly as large as a cow's horn, but wonderful, cream white.

One moment there was quiet, except for the cries of celebration, and the next the clatter of shields and the chime of swords drifted through the smoke. Njord stopped carving and stood, leaning against the side of the ship.

The Spjotmen ran, yelling, some of them bleeding. Their words were harsh and shouted—bellowed. Wiglaf had never known such noisy people. Strong shoulders ran the ship out into the river. Men fell into the ship, speaking excitedly, and Wiglaf cowered.

Sea chests were swung into the ship. They were so heavy that the men grunted with effort, as well as with fury at what was happening. The ship was rocked into the river, and men splashed, shoving the vessel farther into the current. The heavy sea chests unbalanced the ship. Men grunted, fighting the chests into new positions until the ship steadied. The ship worked by sweating, bleeding men, and oars rumbled out through the oar holes.

The ship turned, the strength of the men working it, but there were cries and crashing sounds from the bank. Wiglaf caught the sound of a few English curses, and his pulse quickened. The men of the other ships were not so quick. There were commands, and then the rush of oars in water.

Bowmen stood and loosed arrows toward the bank. An answering spear rang into a shield. The ship yawed with the current, and there were cries everywhere as Wiglaf cringed.

Blood pooled in the ship. Wounds gaped. Men gasped as they rowed. *Raven* had to stay near the other two ships until they were safely into the main current. A man with a badly scarred nose seemed to call out to the attackers that he was not afraid, or that his arrows would kill all of them, or something equally frightening to Wiglaf's ears.

Lidsmod manned an oar too. An arrow sang off a helmet, and he ducked. Another arrow splintered off a shield boss. Men shouted threats toward the riverbank, but it was obvious they were eager to reach the fastest current.

Wiglaf was not happy to see these men hurt. They were in pain, and that made Wiglaf bite his lip in sympathy. Besides, they might remember that Wiglaf was not really one of them and do something terrible to him now.

As the men rowed, the ship began to skim the river. The fighters on the bank, however, seemed to keep pace with the ship. An arrow glanced through the sunlight. Another struck the cross-shaped frame that held the furled sail. The arrow stayed there until a hand snatched it from the wood and snapped it in two.

Gradually the pursuers were left behind. Wiglaf found himself able to look over the sides of the ship. He wanted to call out that he was here, that he was well, but there was no one to call to. The other two ships skimmed the river, and a flock of ducks formed miniature wakes as they swam out of the way. The blood puddles on the oak planks shifted back and forth as the men rowed.

Gunnar struck a sea chest with his fist. "We were caught drunk, pissing into the fire."

"It was everyone's fault," said Njord. "We all should have expected this."

"Why are we running away?" asked Gorm. "We can turn back. We have nothing to be afraid of!"

No one answered him. The ship rode more heavily now. With the gold in its belly, it would not be as seaworthy.

Gorm stopped rowing and stood upright. "I am

ashamed of my village! We run like children at the sight of a few helmets." Blood streamed from under Gorm's helmet and from the gash on his thigh. He did not seem to feel the wounds.

Gunnar ordered the rowing stopped. The men panted, leaning forward to rest.

"Gorm," said Gunnar evenly, "sit down."

Gorm pulled the helmet off his head. His blood was scarlet in the sunlight. Eirik was bleeding from a black puncture in his upper arm. There were other wounds among the men. Opir spat blood into his hand. He worked fingers back into his jaw and removed a broken molar. "I tried to bite a chunk out of a shield, and it didn't taste very good," said Opir.

A few men chuckled. Opir rose weakly, standing by the mast. "Nobody could outrun Gorm, though" said Opir. "He ran ahead of me, and I was running as fast as I could."

Gorm did not laugh. Lidsmod avoided meeting the man's eyes.

"Be happy, Gunnar," said Njord. "We have gold, and we have our lives. Did you think we could burn two villages and not do at least a little real fighting?"

Gunnar was not happy, but there had been worse days under the sun. "We'll have to put some of the gold into *Crane* and *Landwaster*. I don't like the way we're riding." They would let the current and the oars carry them beyond any possible danger, and then they would back oars for as long as it took to redistribute the gold.

Eirik slumped. Trygg supported him, and Opir reached an arm to help him up. Voices encouraged him, but the saga master was pale. When he spoke the lines from the story of the labors of Thor, his voice was a mere whisper. "Therefore I wrestle with Death herself," the poet recited.

"Shoulder to shoulder with the oldest adversary," Lidsmod recited in turn, putting out an arm to the weary poet. Lidsmod was shocked to see the strong man look so suddenly frail.

We would bind the wounds even of our enemy.

The words were Father Aethelwulf's, spoken long ago in the light from a tallow candle. It was like hearing the abbot's actual voice, close and unafraid. Wiglaf considered how Father Aethelwulf would want him to act. If any one of these strangers misunderstood Wiglaf's motives, they would not hesitate to use a sword.

Hesitant at first, Wiglaf told Njord what he wanted to do. The helmsman did not respond. Wiglaf repeated himself with gestures.

Njord's eyes widened. Njord and Lidsmod stared, looked at each other, and Njord ran a hand through his white hair. He smiled doubtfully, and made something like a shrug. Wiglaf could almost understand what he said next. It might be a good idea, it might be bad, said the old man to Lidsmod. Was Wiglaf to be trusted?

There was a moment of indecision.

Njord found his carving knife and handed it to Lidsmod. "Cut him loose," he said. "And get him what he wants."

Lidsmod cut strips of wool from a garment pulled out of a sea chest, and Wiglaf tied them around Eirik's arm, after first making a pad of wool to fit exactly over the wound. Wiglaf had seen Aethelwulf do this many times, and he could sense Aethelwulf's approval from Heaven as he worked. These men were not Wiglaf's friends, but they were hurt.

Eirik smiled wanly. He thanked Wiglaf in a deep, gentle voice.

The men of *Raven* watched. They admired craftsmanship, and Wiglaf's work with a bandage was not the work of a mere boy. This new thrall had the hands of a wise, skilled master.

Wiglaf turned to Gorm. In words that carried unmistakable meaning, the thrall asked Gorm if he could bandage his leg.

Gorm gave no answer. He lifted his hand to strike Wiglaf.

33

"LET HIM BIND YOUR WOUND," SAID GUNNAR.

"A ship full of women," spat Gorm, and he lowered his fist slowly.

But he had watched the boy work and understood that perhaps the thrall had some uncommon value. If he could bind wounds, he might know other medicine lore. He might know plants and mosses, and he might, more important, have that touch that learning cannot bring.

Gorm shook the thrall away from his head. It was nothing, he said. It did not hurt.

For the first time Gorm thought that perhaps he would not kill the thrall. Perhaps the thrall would be more than simply useful. He was young—he could have a long life. Gorm considered how valuable it would be to have a medicine thrall. Hurt and sick people would send to Gorm and ask for help. He would charge them gold—not sheep, not horses, but unalloyed gold. "Three pieces of gold," Gorm would demand. "Three pieces, or my thrall does nothing, and you will die."

This was, Gorm thought, an excellent plan. He would

buy the thrall from his sea mates and then have gold for the rest of his life. Never again would he have to sail with a crew of weak, clumsy men. He could live alone, with his thrall to earn him gold.

To the people of Spjothof, Gorm knew, worth was everything. Without worth, a man was simply a featherless bird. But with worth, he had a place among men and women.

Gunnar gave the order, and men began rowing again. Lidsmod took Eirik's place and struggled to pull as hard as the rest. Afternoon shadows fell across the river. Gunnar watched the banks.

The ships neared the site of their first attack. Keel scars still marked the banks near that first village. It seemed so long ago! The men glanced as they rowed. There was no sign of smoke now. There was no sign at all that there had been a village. Gunnar motioned to Lidsmod, and the thrall's head was kept down. Let the people here imagine that the boy had been burned or drowned or speared, thought Lidsmod. There were men who especially delighted in spearing boys, even infants. Let the villagers imagine the worst.

A single figure ran to the bank and watched them pass.

"I could hit him with an arrow," said Trygg.

"Keep rowing," said Gunnar.

"A windless day like this—it would be easy," Trygg protested without much heart. "A miserable village, that," said Gorm. "Torsten did all the fighting." He said this without much force, however; his mind was on the future. He would be wealthy. He would be seen as kind-hearted.

Gorm dreamed that the jarl himself might be sick one day and ask for his thrall. "For the jarl," Gorm would say, "there will be no price. I give my thrall's services to the jarl." Men would be amazed and impressed. "Gorm is generous as well as brave," they would say.

The river broadened and became more and more like a sea.

Terns squealed along the banks. They were river birds as well as seabirds, but when the gulls appeared, Lidsmod thought hopefully that he could taste salt in the air.

The land here was still. No one pursued them, and Lidsmod believed that they were safe now.

Gunnar signaled to *Crane*. *Crane* in turn signaled to *Landwaster*.

Lidsmod rowed beside Ulf. He had thoughts he could not shake, and the more he thought, the more he believed he was right. He would wait until the right moment, and then he would act.

It was not a plan that needed Thor strength—it was a plan the One-eyed God would understand. Lidsmod knew he could not explain to his sea mates what he intended to do. Perhaps they would never forgive him, and he would be exiled. That would be hard. He would miss his friends, his mother, and Gunnar. But Lidsmod believed that Odin would understand. More than this: he believed Odin wanted it.

The weather vane fluttered in a breeze. It was the day's first wind, but it was in from the sea. Gunnar ordered the ship ashore, and men sprang from *Raven* to drag her to safety.

Lidsmod worked with the rest of the men, hauling *Raven*. He prayed silently to the One-eyed God that he was right.

34

WIGLAF SAT in the midst of a bustling camp.

He worked at being small, certain that if any one of these men really saw him, actually perceived his dark hair and darting eyes and his annoying littleness, his throat would be cut. They would not even mean harm by it, he thought. It would be like squashing a tick.

Wiglaf had begun to wonder if some of these men might be kind. Some certainly appeared friendly. But he also sensed that if the ships traveled much farther, they would be on the sea. He had seen unfamiliar birds, with dark heads and white bodies, and smelled the salty, freshening scent in the air rivermen referred to when they described the ocean. Wiglaf did not want to sail the sea. He did not want to go far away with these strangers. But his home was destroyed, and everyone, including Father Aethelwulf, had been killed, he was sure. Wiglaf shrank, wishing he were invisible.

Gunnar sniffed. He glanced at Lidsmod and held a finger to his lips.

Lidsmod thought he could nose landsmen if they were anywhere near. They smelled like sheep and pig and old rancid fat, as well as cheese and boiled beef. He drew in a long breath through his nostrils. If an army of the unwashed wanted to attack, they would rush from the trees. These very trees around the camp.

Gunnar rubbed his hands together and blew into them because there was a chill. Lidsmod squeezed his shield grip and was surprised at how sore his palm was. He had held the shield tightly during the battle, and in his inexperience was surprised at the stiffness in his arms and back.

To Lidsmod's surprise, Gunnar asked him, "What do you think the landsmen will do?"

"Watch us carefully," Lidsmod said, feeling honored. "Observe us from a distance."

The forest was a mass of black tree skeletons, just furred with leaf. The unwashed knew how to hide, and how to sneak up on a group of very weary seamen. Let them attack, thought Lidsmod. Let them try. He would welcome one last chance to test his sword.

And then he laughed at himself.

It wasn't true, this hunger for fighting. He wished for the music of sea waves, sea wind. Lidsmod had river grit under his nails, and his knuckles were grimy with pitch from the new ship. His hair was stiff with silt and sweat. He ached for the next bath day—when hot water would ease him and he would feel cleansed of this land.

"You don't think they'll attack?" asked Gunnar. His long hair was gathered neatly behind his head, fastened with a leather clasp, but there was a shadow of weariness under each eye.

Lidsmod realized it was a question that tested more than his ability to predict the near future. Gunnar was weighing Lidsmod's judgment, his power to predict what these unfamiliar men might do.

The wind whispered out of the east. It sang through the branches near the river and struggled with the river current, tossing small river waves. It tugged at Lidsmod's dirty hair and at his cloak. The wind smelled dry, and was steady rather than strong. Clouds tumbled slowly in the twilight, and the ships lay just out of reach of the surging water.

"I don't know," said Lidsmod at last.

Gunnar gave a satisfied syllable of affirmation. Somehow Lidsmod had given the right answer.

The tide would be going out soon, but it would not help the men of Spjothof. Gunnar explained that it was unwise to head into the sea against a stiff wind. Unless the wind shifted soon, they would have to spend the night here.

Men lifted sea chests and staggered from ship to ship. The gold was evenly distributed among the three vessels. The three leadmen also discussed the deployment of guards. They decided on twenty guards, to be replaced throughout the night. There would be no more mistakes.

Lidsmod hesitated. Do I dare to tell Gunnar my plan? He was standing beside the leadman, the forest trees stretching black branches through the late-day sky.

Lidsmod's mother had keened the old songs, tales of gods and dwarves. Suffering was exchanged for peace, pain for solace. Lidsmod tried to believe that Gunnar would understand.

"Gunnar, good neighbor," Lidsmod said. Nothing gave more honor than the respectful use of a man's name. "Do you know what my mother would want us to do?"

174

"Regarding what?" asked Gunnar, watching the forest and the sunset-gold river.

Lidsmod wished he could have a future with Wiglaf. The boy was very nearly a companion. He thought Wiglaf understood much of what was said. He wished he could show Wiglaf how to play the board game every man and boy loved—*hnefatafl*—a game for long winter nights beside fires.

He could show him how to use his king in a position of strength so that he would win, always. Or nearly always. They could roll the walrus-ivory die and see whose luck was strongest. He could lend Wiglaf his elk-bone ice skates, or perhaps ask Njord to make a pair so that Wiglaf could race with him across the fjord.

Lidsmod groped in his tunic and found what he wanted. He extended it toward Wiglaf. The thrall's eyes were bright, but he did not take it at once.

"For you," said Lidsmod.

Wiglaf's eyes asked a question.

"A gift."

The thrall's hands were not tied, but he was seated beside a stump at the center of the camp, his feet tangled in a hobble of walrus-leather thongs. This was the same kind of device that kept horses from trotting off in the night.

Wiglaf would have had trouble with these knots. Njord had tied them, and each knot was a separate secret. Njord knew all the knots, from the dwarf knot to the savior knot, the one for a man swept out of a ship and into the sea. Knotted inextricably in the hobble was a small iron bell that jingled prettily every time Wiglaf moved.

The boy's hand hesitated, then closed around the gift. Wiglaf smiled and thanked Lidsmod in his strange tongue.

Wiglaf ran his fingers over a comb made of bone. It was carved with beautiful markings, like a row of flying gulls. The teeth were sturdy and precisely crafted. These strangers could do magic with their knives. Wiglaf ran the comb through his hair so Lidsmod would know that he understood what it was. He thanked him again and tucked the comb away.

"Antler," said Lidsmod. He imitated a deer for a moment, his hands like branches above his head. "Carved from a deer's antler."

A shadow flowed over the earth in the firelight, and the bloody muzzle of a deer grazed the grass, carried into the camp by a hunter. Gunnar had sent Gorm to hunt along with Trygg and two men from *Crane*. Lidsmod was not pleased to see Gorm back so soon.

Gorm knelt and tested Wiglaf's hobble. The man's hands were blood sticky. He tested the thongs. "This is what's keeping him here?" he snapped at Lidsmod. "He could untie himself and hop off like a rabbit."

Lidsmod pointed out the bell. "Every time he stirs, the bell rings."

Wiglaf drew in his feet at just that moment, and the chime sounded.

"I have a much better idea," said Gorm. "One that will keep our little thrall right where he belongs."

35

AFTER GORM HAD BUTCHERED the deer, and the blood and hair was rinsed off in the river, he found a stick among the river stones. He worked a hole at either end of the stick, and asked Njord for some leather thongs.

Njord sat in *Raven,* carving the walrus tooth. "You like to keep your hands busy, Gorm. So do I," he said without looking up.

"It's to keep the thrall safe," said Gorm, trying to disguise his impatience. Njord was a good helmsman and could sail as well as any man, but sometimes he was as slow-witted as any other villager.

Njord glanced at the stick in Gorm's hands. "We don't want Wiglaf running off, do we?" said Njord.

Gorm did not want to hear that the thrall had a name. Gorm would give the thrall a name when he had paid for him. A good, powerful name. Perhaps simply *Gormsthrall*.

Gorm fastened Wiglaf's hands behind him. He tied the stick between Wiglaf's wrists. He wrapped the straps until Wiglaf gasped. Gorm laughed in what he assumed was a soothing manner.

"Don't worry, your hands won't drop off." Gorm smiled. "This little span will keep your hands apart. You can't untie your knots now." He patted Wiglaf on the head. "Wiglaf," he said, struggling with the ridiculous name. "Good Wiglaf, the thrall of Gorm. A good servant and helper," he added.

Wiglaf gave him something like a smile.

Ulf threw an armload of half-rotten firewood to the ground and asked Lidsmod to help him. "There is much more than I can carry," he said. Ulf beckoned him to the place where the birch logs were stacked. "I need your help with more than firewood," said Ulf, when Lidsmod reached him.

Lidsmod had never heard Ulf speak in such a furtive manner before. His voice was low and quiet, and he glanced around them as he spoke. A blackbird made bright music high above them, and Ulf looked up as though the bird might overhear something it should not.

"I am telling you a secret," said Ulf, putting a fist over his heart. "A blood secret."

Lidsmod was flattered that Ulf would share such a secret with him, but he was mystified. "Ulf, please tell me—is anything wrong?"

"Swear, before the gods, that you will keep this between us."

This was very serious. Lidsmod had never made such a formal promise in his life. "I so swear."

"I am going to let little Leg Biter go free."

Lidsmod did not respond.

"The thrall," said Ulf. "I will let him escape."

Lidsmod tried to read Ulf's features. This had been Lidsmod's hope as well, and while Gunnar had not agreed at once, he had not chided Lidsmod for daring to offer such a scheme. "Let me consider it," was all Gunnar had said.

"The boy gave us his gift when he bound Eirik's wound," Ulf continued. "That was a bad wound and might have bled until Eirik died. I think the thrall saved Eirik's life." Odin thought was hard, and few men could do it. When men heard such talk, they tended to respect it.

"He repaid us for saving his life when we kept him from drowning. And I think we should give him a last gift. Besides," Ulf continued, "Odin crippled him when he was born, or when he was still an infant. That means he belongs to the gods. We have to let the boy go. The others will understand when it's done. I'll pay for the thrall after he's gone."

Lidsmod felt a flash of admiration and even love for Ulf.

"My thoughts walk with yours," said Lidsmod, the old saying that meant complete agreement. "But I think Gorm will slice our heads from our necks."

36

WIGLAF SLEPT, despite the laughter around him, and the sounds of boasting and wild tales. Gradually the camp settled. New guards cast shadows across sleeping men as they took their places at the edge of the firelight.

Someone whispered; there was a step in the sand at his ear. This was the moment Wiglaf had feared. One of these men crouched beside him, knife in hand.

Wiglaf woke, sure it was only a nightmare. But it was not a nightmare. A killer knelt over him. And that bright knife glinted in his hand, eager to be sticky with Wiglaf's blood. Wiglaf tried to scream but he had no air. He could not move.

Then came some soft speech, and a gentle hand touched his shoulder. Lidsmod said something kind and covered Wiglaf's lips with his fingers. "Don't worry," he seemed to say.

Firelight fluttered from the last charred logs. Men snored. Guards stood, looking away from the river, toward the forest.

Ulf's knife was red in the firelight. The knife bit through the hobble and slashed the bindings Gorm had contrived. Ulf's hands were quick, stripping the leather from Wiglaf's ankles and wrists. Ulf smiled and stuffed moss into the iron bell. Lidsmod and the stout, bald-headed man pulled Wiglaf to his feet.

They led him to the river.

Two guards watched over the ships, and these men lowered spears toward Wiglaf.

"What is this, Ulf?" asked one of the guards.

"Watch. I'll show you." He turned to Wiglaf. He gestured, his voice low. "Run, Wiglaf. Run home. Go quickly." He slapped Wiglaf's back. "Run now!"

Wiglaf started, and stopped.

"Hurry!" Ulf said.

The two spearmen stepped toward Wiglaf, but he danced away.

As he ran he heard an iron bell chiming, far off on the other side of the camp. Lidsmod! He was running in the opposite direction, drawing pursuers away from Wiglaf.

There were shouts. These strangers had the fiercest voices! Wiglaf nearly fell at the sound. But he told himself: I will not stumble.

Wiglaf splashed into water for a moment, and veered. The river was nearly at his feet, but he could not climb through the wall of tree trunks at his right. He ran until tears streamed, and then collided with a tree in the dark. He forced himself up, through the claws of branches, the stalks of hazel wood and the teeth of brambles, up into the forest. There was starlight, and the dullest moon.

Suddenly branches crashed behind him, and breath hissed into his ear.

"I have you!" said Gorm.

Gorm's teeth were bright. His hands clutched Wiglaf's tunic, then his leg, then fumbled at Wiglaf's heel.

Wiglaf slithered. He leaped and ran hard into a tree. He rebounded, and dived into shrubs he could not even see, hoping they would be thick enough to hide him. Hadn't he always been Wiglaf the spider?

Gorm's hand closed around his foot. Wiglaf struggled to hang on to something with his stronger hand, but the man was much too powerful for him. Wiglaf felt stalks and leaves break between his fingers. He could not find a handhold among this young growth.

Gorm laughed, panting.

Wiglaf bit him. He did not know what limb he was biting exactly, although as his teeth sank and blood filled his mouth, he surmised that it was one of Gorm's arms. The man gasped, struck Wiglaf on the head, and flung him into the air.

Wiglaf sailed through the darkness. He fell into a cradle of branches and landed on his feet.

Gorm was just behind him. Once he felt Gorm's fingertips graze his shoulder and Wiglaf fell deliberately; he rolled through squelching mossy mud and then ran again. Hares don't run in a straight line, stone to wall to tree. They slant, swivel, scamper, and then, to cheat the hound, they run straight for awhile. Wiglaf raced one way, then another, and Gorm's hand snatched at air just past Wiglaf's ear. Wiglaf dodged, and then he was a rabbit, indeed.

This was Wiglaf the hare, and Gorm ran hard, slogging through the wet branches and splashing through puddles, but Wiglaf seemed to avoid the puddles—or perhaps there was a charm in his running that night. Perhaps the puddles shifted to avoid Wiglaf, and found Gorm's feet instead. Forests are not simple places. They lie beyond the word and ken of humans, and Wiglaf ran afraid of the trees around him as much as he feared Gorm.

There came a moment during the running when Wiglaf realized he was alone. Gorm was no longer behind him. The forest was silent around him, closing in, trees leaning over him with their great, dark heads.

At last Wiglaf walked. His breath thundered and his heart galloped, so he could not discern what was forest sound and what was the noise of his own body. He could not tell if Gorm followed him at a distance. He could hear nothing but himself. His nose was streaming, and he forced himself onward. He realized that he did not know where he was going.

He was lost, swallowed by forest. He hurried along what looked like a path, and then he realized that there was light. It was a poor, thumb-worn daylight, but it was not darkness. Birds answered each other, and Wiglaf worked his way along the path, praying that it paralleled the river. So long as Wiglaf knew where the river was, he was not lost.

But the river was nowhere. Forest slime glistened at his feet. There were trees, furry and green in places, smooth and sere in others. There were stones scaled and blistered with lichen. Tree-colored birds scurried, pin-sharp beaks and quick eyes all around him.

Wiglaf kept to the path. No one had walked this trail for many years, he believed. This path was a bad charm, the way into a witch's embrace.

37

AS THE SUN ROSE, Wiglaf found the river. Or perhaps the path found it, or the river found Wiglaf. The dawn-bright water was sliced by the black trunks of trees. But it was an old friend, this river—Wiglaf knew where he was. He climbed behind a tree, exhausted, and prayed that Saint Peter would stand guard and let no harm find him.

He slept.

Wiglaf woke thirsty, hungry, and frightened. He hurried to look at the river. It was still morning. The current was busy and had more color now.

He ran again, but he did not run fast. It was a trot, like the pace a dog might try to maintain over distance. He had never dreamed that there were so many trees. This river no longer looked so much like the way home.

He walked all day, and at night he slept hard, dreamlessly.

It was when the earth turned gray that Wiglaf realized the sun was rising again. It was another day. But he had forgotten the names for things in his hunger and weariness.

He had forgotten his own name. He had forgotten where he was going, or where he had been. He knew only Going and Walking, one step after another. He would walk forever.

That was when he saw the wolf.

Like all such creatures, it was beautiful, and yet with the sort of beauty the eyes can scarcely believe. And it was following him, its slanted eyes invisible in the first light. It had long legs and silver-brown fur. It nosed forward, following Wiglaf more quickly as Wiglaf began to pant.

Wiglaf was shocked back into knowing. Where one wolf ran, dozens followed. Soon a wolf company would fill the path behind Wiglaf, and they would trot closer and closer, wolf slather flowing. There would be a mead hall of wolves. Wiglaf looked back every few paces and each time he looked the beast was closer. Its eyes were black, like fine nicks taken with a knife, not at all the open gaze of Stag.

The wolf was near now. Wiglaf sobbed, breaking into a shaky trot. He did not have the strength to run any faster. The animal was nearer yet, closing on him. When the path turned, the wolf disappeared for a moment, keeping to a straight line, reappearing when the path no longer crooked.

Wiglaf fumbled for a stone. He found one and flung it at the creature. The wolf lifted one paw and sniffed at the rock. He looked back at Wiglaf, his mouth open in a carnivorous grin.

At that moment, a bear climbed through the forest.

Wiglaf would never be certain about this. When he

thought back on it later, there had been, he knew, a wolf. But the bear had not been like a bear at all, and Wiglaf would wonder as long as he lived what, in fact, had approached through the woods that morning.

It was huge, too big to be real, but it crackled the leaves and shoved saplings to one side. It stayed beyond the trees, so Wiglaf could only see its shadow—the size of an ale hall—where it rose and fell.

The wolf hesitated and whined. The bear snapped twigs, just out of sight. The wolf stepped sideways and sniffed again, and its muzzled wrinkled. The wolf bared its white teeth and growled.

Wiglaf scrambled down the path, and the bear grew closer, its slow paws crushing leaves, its breath chuffing in the cold morning. Or was it the spirit of all dead bears trailing him through the forest? Or a bear of magic, of divine power, come after Wiglaf to protect him? Sometimes it clambered ahead, and Wiglaf could just see the shag of his back fur above the bushes.

The bear stayed with Wiglaf and did not leave him. All day the great animal accompanied him on his journey. Wiglaf spoke to it, but he would never be able to recall what he said to it, or why it seemed that the bear answered.

Wiglaf approached the landmark and did not know it. He was not seeing the world anymore; he was only walking. Breath came out of him, a silent cry, and he stopped. *I know this place.*

It was the *aldwark,* the stone ruin beside the road.

But it couldn't be. Surely he had not traveled far

enough yet, he thought. Sun spilled through the trees. Birds lifted their voices, like the broken voices of children. Wiglaf would walk forever, he believed. Stride after stride—it was all he had ever done. Now he was walking to the place he remembered, but of course it was all burned to ashes, and all the people were gone.

The familiar one-two note of a cuckoo drifted from across an empty field. Scattered sheep droppings and sheep-cropped grass stretched all the way to the forest. The flock was gone. He took a breath to call out the name of his dog, but of course there was no familiar dog—nothing living remained.

His legs collapsed and he lay still on the soft earth of the road. He would rise again soon and trudge the road through the charred places where his mother and father had lived, and his brothers, and Aethelwulf.

Wiglaf wondered if this was what it was like to die—warm sun kneading his body, a voice calling his name.

38

GORM RETURNED ALONG the riverbank slowly and quietly. He had believed that someday he would sit beside the quick, stunning-cold white water and be happy.

He had believed that Gormsthrall would bring him stature and honor, and that the years ahead would be kind. When the men from Heglund, a village of rich pig farmers, docked and traded stories over mead, Gorm would sit upright among them, his silent pride better than any boast.

Now he did not need to hurry. He was deliberate and careful. His future had fled, and he would seek out the man who had caused it to depart. And kill him.

The fire danced, and men crouched or stood near it, the shadows quaking. Gorm stepped into the circle of light. Ulf sat with his hands folded, a sleepy look in his eyes as his gaze met Gorm's.

Good, steady Ulf, thought Gorm. The man everyone trusts.

"Stand up," said Gorm in a quiet voice.

Ulf stood from his place beside Lidsmod. The young man forced himself to stand too, his legs stiff from rowing. Ulf said the old justice formula, "Right for wrong, I will pay for your loss in gold."

Men leaned forward. This was only proper, and they were not surprised that Ulf wanted to pay for what he had done. Ulf was a worthy man. They were relieved that Ulf realized that the loss of this thrall was a loss for all of them. A thrall with knowledge of medicine would have fetched a high price from the Swedes or from a jarl in another village.

"You all know me well," Ulf continued, "as you knew my father and my uncles. You know the men and the women of my family always pay what they owe."

Men murmured. This was true.

"Tell us why you did it," urged Njord.

"Yes," hissed Gorm. His voice was like sticks breaking. "I want to know why you did it too, and I will listen with great interest."

"I will pay," Ulf said. He spoke quietly, but spoke into the soul of every man there. "Because Odin has given us good fortune. And because the thrall, little Leg Biter—Wiglaf—had lost the strength of one arm and was not ours to keep. He belongs to the gods." Ulf used high speech, the language of challenges and formal contracts.

"This is madness," Gorm spat. "No one believes such froth about Odin and the gods. Nobody listens to that sort of talk—that's for children around hearthfires. We're men, Ulf. I do not accept your gold. I demand a greater payment."

Lidsmod shook inwardly at these words. This was close to a formal challenge.

"You seek my life?" asked Ulf. His voice was quiet, as though they sat on a pleasant afternoon in the sun.

189

"Maybe some of our shipmates," said Gorm, "dream about Odin as much as Ulf does. I don't. I piss on the gods. Step forward, Ulf. I challenge you before all this company to fight to the death."

Ulf shook his shoulders and cocked his head back and forth like a man stirring from a nap—Ulf's way, his friends knew, of hiding his apprehension. A brave man sometimes had to disguise his fear, sometimes with a laugh, sometimes with affected complacency. Gorm was very nearly the most dangerous fighter in Spjothof, and even a stout warrior like Ulf would stand little chance.

Ulf said nothing more to Gorm but slowly drew Long and Sharp from its scabbard. He called the name of this fine sword, the result of highest dwarf craft. *"Langhvass!"* he said, speaking softly to his blade. "Sword of my fathers, stand with me in this dark night!"

This was a classic war prayer, and the words turned in each man. They did not want to watch this last fight of such a good sea mate. Lidsmod glanced at Gunnar and saw that the chief was tempted to step in. Gunnar's hand was on his own sword, but he did not want to shame Ulf before all these men. The old harpoon scar was livid on Gunnar's cheek, and Lidsmod understood how hard it was to lead men.

Lidsmod put his hand on his own hilt and stepped forward into the firelight. "And you will have to fight me too," he said, adding, in the ancient saga phrase, "though it cost me blood and breath." His voice was ragged, but he knew the words were correct.

Eirik leaped between them, his bandaged arm a reminder of the lost thrall. "Lidsmod and Ulf do not owe any of us a life."

Gorm snorted. "If they choose not to fight me, I will accept thirty sheep in payment."

Ulf and Lidsmod had no sheep. Gorm knew this. All Ulf had was his share of the gold, and his life, and Lidsmod was a new shield man, who had never settled a farm. Every word now, and every gesture, was borrowed from the sagas. The challenge, even Eirik's attempt to prevent the fight before it began, were all from one ancient song or another, and Gorm and Ulf were now trapped in the Norns' web, in the net of myth and fate.

Gorm kicked aside a charred knot of wood. His sword flickered in the firelight. He smiled with teeth like gold and beckoned Ulf forward like an adversary in a battle poem.

Gorm's sword swept easily and bit blue fire from Ulf's blade. The clash made every man start and creep backward, away from the fire. In song, real steel does not bite steel, nor do real men sweat in firelight as Ulf was sweating, despite his calm smile. Gorm smiled too and lunged, feinted, and struck sparks again. Ulf circled, blocking two more blows, but Gorm was toying with him, teasing, Gorm's shadow like a second Gorm, helping him, leaning forward to spy a weakness.

Neither man had a shield. Neither man had a helmet, nor did each wear armor. Lidsmod waited, sword in hand, for his turn to taste the keen edge. The fighting men wore only wool, the gray cloth of their village. Gorm faked, lunged, feinted, and then Ulf fought off a series of blows toward his face, the white blade of Gorm ringing off Long and Sharp. Dancing around Ulf, Gorm showed why he was feared.

Ulf was slow. He struck back, but as his sword was

raised it was plain that Ulf knew it would not come close to Gorm, and it did not. Ulf was powerful, legs and arms, but his strength was against him now—he was not quick enough.

The blades were lengths of firelight, spans of heat that spat sparks, and yet it was Gorm who crept ever nearer, and it was Gorm whose leg snaked behind Ulf, and the big man was down. Gorm was on him, his hand reaching to grip Ulf's hair for an easy throat cut, but Ulf struck Gorm on the side of the head, and Gorm sprawled face down in the sand.

Gorm stood, brushing the white grains from his smile and spat. Lidsmod felt his heart shrivel.

"He's right." A white-haired figure stepped between them, holding out his arms to embrace Gorm. "He's right," repeated Njord. The interruption in the combat was welcome but startling, an act not rooted in poetry or battle lore. "He doesn't owe us anything, not even gold. Wiglaf paid for his freedom by binding our cuts, Gorm."

"That's true," said Eirik, eager to support Njord even in this break from protocol. "No one wants blood."

"This fighting is needless, Gorm," said Njord.

"Are there no men here?" asked Gorm, looking around at the firelit faces. "Are there no strong men here at all?"

Gorm struck Njord fiercely with the pommel of his sword.

39

THE BLOW WAS QUICK.

The men groaned as Njord fell, face hard into the sand, a starfish of blood spreading in his white hair. Men stared, unable to move or think, anguished to see the blood of this fine seaman, who once carved a serpent from the tusk of a narwhal, and whose steady hand seemed to cup the stars and count them each night.

"Njord!" cried Lidsmod. He fell to his knees beside his old friend, the master of wind. "Njord, get up," Lidsmod implored, bending over the helmsman where he lay.

Gorm did a thing no saga prescribed. Men took in a hard breath as they saw it. Lifting his sword over Lidsmod as he knelt beside the bleeding shipwright, Gorm steadied himself for the deathblow. Lidsmod saw the sword about to fall but stayed right where he was, kneeling protectively over his friend.

There was a snarl, and a shape burst through the dark.

Torsten grappled with Gorm. Gorm wrestled, clawed, tried to slash with his sword, but the unarmed Torsten, clad only in his bear shirt, hammered Gorm with both fists. Blood streamed from Gorm's face. Torsten roared and smashed Gorm with the bear god's fury.

The sound of Torsten's fists was sickening. Gorm's face was a scarlet mass by the time Gunnar and Eirik had their arms around the berserker. None of the other men stepped forward, unwilling to interfere in a moment when a god was present among them.

The two wrestled with Torsten until Gunnar cried out, asking for help. Then the others joined in. It was a long struggle, but at last Torsten was bound and the bear roar was silenced.

The berserker was bright with Gorm's blood. "Gorm said he pissed on the gods."

No one spoke.

"Did I—" Torsten coughed. "Did I hurt him?"

Gunnar put an arm around him. "Sleep, Torsten. Go with these men and sleep in the ship."

"Did I hurt him?" asked the anguished Torsten.

Gorm died before dawn.

What we are dissolves in the eyes of men when we die, Lidsmod knew. A stubborn enemy becomes an honored memory, and a contrary spirit becomes a solemn absence when life is spent. Just as a blood eagle alters an enemy chief into a prize for the gods, so Gorm's death changed him from the man they had known.

His shipmates grieved, brave men who had known Gorm since childhood. Gorm's soul had been a labyrinth, a long fjord with many turnings. But now he was beloved for all his knotty nature. Never again would they see him stepping out from a forest with his prey.

Floki wept most bitterly. Gorm's faults were easy to forget now that his eyes had closed forever. Floki would give Gorm all his sheep back. He did not want the horse price. He wanted Gorm—sneaky, untrustworthy, quick-footed Gorm.

Lidsmod, like the others, felt the weight of this death. He felt the taste of it. He knew that Gorm had only himself to blame, but it was a bad thing to lose a man.

Who could make men out of a stick, or a scoop of mud? No one. Men could not be carved out of ivory or worked out of bone. They came out of air and went back into air, a mystery.

Eirik sang the song of Heimdall, the enigmatic god who had made men. The song was what each man needed to hear at this moment. Men were an accident, an afterthought, beloved of very little. Did the sky love men? Did the sea? Did the surf off the rocky shore love men?

Only men loved men. They wrapped their shipmate in sealskin. They would not burn his bones in this unclean land. They would take his remains to Spjothof, where he could be mourned among his neighbors.

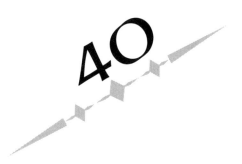

ÆTHELWULF SWEPT the ruined sanctuary clean of all ash, but now the wind had turned and the ash was blowing back again. He was like a man sweeping back the sea. The charred bits scurried around his feet and swirled.

The broom fell apart, a mere stick in his hands. The parts of the broom scattered, twig and cord. He gave a weary laugh, and bent over to gather them up. He sat in a corner doing a good job, he thought, of repairing the bundled straw. Now that he had it in his lap, he could see that it had suffered from fire like everything else. Fire came. Wind blew. Man did what he could. To work was to pray.

Lente, lente, he told himself. *Semper lente.* Slowly, slowly. Always slowly. To lose is to have. He had been a smart, ill-tempered young man. Now he was a loving, ill-tempered old man.

Wiglaf staggered across the ashy earth with a bucket. Water slopped. Crook-jawed Stag trotted in behind him. The old dog had stayed in the woods until the day after the new sheep-fold was finished, as though only the sound of ewes and lambs could call the dog to his home.

196

Or perhaps it was the sound of Wiglaf's voice, back among them, gathered in from the road.

"Put the bucket anyplace," said Aethelwulf. "Quickly," he added kindly, "while there is still some water left in it."

Something dropped from Wiglaf's tunic and spun across the floor. A line of thin white fangs grinned at Aethelwulf from the ashes. He picked up the object and ran his finger over the teeth.

"It's a comb, made from an antler," said Wiglaf.

"Indeed?" said Aethelwulf politely, handing it back.

A step at the door made them both turn. Redwald was dressed in a riding cloak, but now he carried a long sword at his belt. Wiglaf knew that Redwald had tarried here, gathering men, taking his time; he rode all the way down-river only after the strangers had ample time to sail away. Redwald was brave enough, but cat smart.

Wiglaf mourned Edwin and his father, but Aethelwulf had counseled that it was a blessing that Forni and his mother were still very much alive. The sight of Lord Redwald disturbed Wiglaf, the nobleman gaunt and bleary-eyed.

"And what charm craft do you have in your hand, Wiglaf?" asked Redwald, accepting a cup of new ale.

"A gift," said Wiglaf. "From the hand of one of the strangers."

"Cast it," Redwald commanded, "into the fire."

Wiglaf looked to Aethelwulf.

"Wiglaf's life was spared," said the abbot. "This gift reminds us of their mercy."

"I will have no reminder of any of those heathen men in my presence," said Redwald. Neighbors said that Redwald wandered the ruined village at night, standing guard over the charred timbers of his ale hall.

Aethelwulf took the cunning object and, with a swirl of his robe, made a gesture, the fire spitting and smoking within its ring of stones.

Wiglaf nearly cried out, but kept his silence at a glance from the abbot.

"It's only right," said Redwald, "that we suffer no remnant of them among us."

"Indeed Redwald," said Aethelwulf. "It is as you wish."

The red-haired nobleman stared into the fire with what looked like real regret. "It is just," he said. He offered a sad smile in Wiglaf's direction, firelight glittering in his eyes.

Later that night, Aethelwulf lay a hand on Wiglaf's shoulder. "Let it remind us," said Aethelwulf, "of our blessings." He pressed the comb into Wiglaf's hand.

Aethelwulf then uttered a prayer, but this was holy speech nothing like any Wiglaf knew. It was a prayer in farm talk, not in Latin—in the language of women at the well, in the tongue of shepherds. It was glorious, but so unusual that Wiglaf did not know whether to say amen after the poem speech was finished, or make the sign of the cross, or simply wait to hear what the abbot would say next.

Wiglaf nearly asked, "Did the Lord God hear such words, and understand them?"

"Tomorrow," said Aethelwulf after a long silence, "you will help me write the words down."

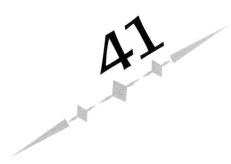

41

THE WIND SLACKENED, and the men ran out the oars.

Gorm's body lay stitched into sealskin. Within its sealskin enclosure Gorm wore his sword and his helmet. His shield hung over the side of the ship, as though Gorm still manned an oar.

Raven had done well, Lidsmod knew. *Raven* would never be as famous as *Landwaster,* but Lidsmod thought that *Landwaster* had not won further glory on this voyage. The old ship leaked, and it was time she sailed only in songs around night fires.

Njord kept a steady hand on the steering oar. His head was bandaged and hurt if he looked into the sunlight off the water. But it was a good pain, he said. He was alive and healing.

Opir had been silent for three days. Now he leaped off his sea chest and announced that he would walk the oars. "I can do this better than any man!" he cried.

It was possible to do this with practice, but the men of Spjothof believed that any man who walked the oars as they stood horizontal from a ship, especially in midocean, was demonstrating wicked pride as well as skill.

Opir knew this. He thrust out his chest in mockery

of his own vanity. "I am the bravest. I am the man with the quickest eyes. I am the man with the smartest feet."

Opir sprang onto the first oar, Floki's. "Eirik cannot do this," called Opir. "Trygg Two-nose cannot do this."

He stepped onto Trygg's oar, and then he spread his arms. He was losing his balance, arms wheeling. But he did not fall. He swayed, arms stretched, and balanced himself.

Opir fell into the sea just as the wind rose, then swam alongside the ship. He called out that it was cold.

Lidsmod reached far over the side, helped by other shipmates, and pulled the shivering boaster into the ship.

The wind swelled the sail and the men shipped their oars. The two following ships began to recede into the distance as *Raven* reached upward, her prow skimming sky as she cut through the living ocean.

The wake was wide, clear, like sword steel.

Eirik began a song, an old tune, the story of a great ship full of treasure. The saga ship winged homeward bearing its gold lightly. But the tune had new words, because now this new ship—*Raven*—was nameworthy, sang Eirik. Her name was newly crafted by the poet into something more proud, fit to be carried to all who heard tales during long winter nights.

Lidsmod climbed back to Njord and took the steering oar. The old man gave up the helm with a show of reluctance, and at first the ship shifted, a current of uncertainty running along her keel. But at last Lidsmod steadied the ship, and under the strength of a following wind, guided the course of *Raven of the Waves.*